THE OVERRIDING MIRACLE

THE OVERRIDING MIRACLE

R HAROLD BROWN

Lighthouse
eBooks

This book is dedicated to my family who love me without fail, a circle of friends who read my story with encouragement, and members of Tuckston United Methodist Church who inspire me.

THE OVERRIDING MIRACLE

Copyright © Harold Brown 2007

This book is a work of fiction. Names, places, characters and incidents are the product of the author's imagination. Any resemblance to actual events or places or persons, living or dead, is entirely coincidental. Facts about the probability of conception are real.

Published by
Lighthouse Christian Publishing
SAN 257-4330
5531 Dufferin Drive
Savage, Minnesota, 55378
United States of America

www.lighthouseebooks.com
www.lighthousechristianpublishing.com

R Harold Brown

Heritage

When he came from the nursing home, Clarence Harris went through all the rooms in the house to see if everything was in order. He found almost nothing out of place. But when he came near the hidden stairway to the attic, he hesitated. He'd not been up here in years.

The old door into the attic opened with the familiar creaking sound that brought back memories of happier times. This was no longer his world, it was his mother's. Maybe a place of her secrets.

With a feeling close to guilt, Clarence studied the mysterious shapes of items stored in the shadows, wondering how long since his mother, or anyone else had been up here. The undisturbed dust looked as if it had been many years since anyone had moved a thing. Although the stair was not hard to get to, this hidden world had remained untouched. Clarence, himself, had not been up here in at least ten years.

Clarence Harris was a man of his time, rising with the tide of American economic and social progress from the middle to the end of the twentieth century. He was not a widely known personality, but he was an educated man. By today's standards he was not wealthy, but certainly not poor. He lived in a nice neighborhood of comfortable houses and half-acre lots with neatly manicured lawns. He and his wife Susan loved their home of the last twenty-five years, and spent much of their Saturdays keeping it up.

As Clarence's eyes adjusted to the dim lighting, he became aware of boxes covered with dust and cobwebs. He hadn't come prepared for the job. He had gotten word from a neighbor that his mother was seriously ill. In fact, she had suffered a stroke serious enough to confine her to the hospital for three weeks. Now she was in a nursing home, not recognizing even those she had known and loved. Clarence had just come from there, feeling terrible for his mother.

He had never seen her sick, except when bedridden with the flu, and probably the occasional day with some other illness when he was young. The drawn look of her expressionless face had shocked him. Lying on her back with her ashen, gaunt face nestled in white hair pressed deep into the pillow, she was more of a stranger than mother. Clarence had never seen her look so old and lifeless. The smile that always came when he appeared was absent. The only hint of emotion was a fear in her eyes that seemed to deepen when he asked her questions.

"How you feeling, Mama," he had said, trying to keep his voice steady. "Are you comfortable? Can I get you something? Would you like me to read to you? I have your Bible here."

None of these questions had brought any response. Clarence read a few pages from Psalms, some of her favorite verses, but he couldn't keep his voice under control. He decided he was doing more harm than good, especially to himself.

He had sat by the bed with his eyes closed — he didn't know how long — remembering when this lady, who could no longer react, was the source and light of his life. Perhaps he didn't appreciate it fully back then, but he was now recounting as many of those gifts as possible. And the unfolding memories were both therapy and agony. His mother was constantly concerned for his comfort and happiness; she always had a snack for him when he got home from school, always a hug when he left and returned. He gave these things no thought back then, except to be embarrassed when his friends noticed her affection. She was just as steady in her praise when he succeeded, as in her pressure when he dawdled. Now his mother's lifelong attention seemed a great gift, a deciding factor in the direction of his life. It seemed unbearable that she could no longer encourage him. Worse, he could not tell her how much her support had meant — the adult orphan's burden.

He had sat with her for the whole morning today, and most of yesterday, and met several of her neighbors and church members who came to see how she was. Some were people he knew from childhood, but most were only vaguely familiar because he'd not seen them in thirty-plus years. He explained all he knew about his mother's condition a dozen times, and suffered along with each of the visitors the sudden failure of a beloved mother whom they all praised easily and lavishly.

And now here he was in her house, coming to check on the things he would likely have to take care of soon. There was so much to be attended to: bank accounts, house care, insurance, bills to be paid and relatives to notify. With some guilt he kept thinking of work awaiting him back home. He missed Susan, and was glad that she would be here the day after tomorrow after she finished with the church garage sale that she had been organizing for weeks.

Well, where to start on the items in front of him? Most of the boxes were labeled, which made the decision easier. Some large ones were marked *Clothes*, some *Toys*, some *Misc*. After standing in silence, Clarence was beginning to have second thoughts about looking at anything in the attic today. He should be downstairs, where he would likely find all the documents and items he needed to put his mother's current affairs in order. Why was he up here anyway? Nothing had been put in this attic in a long time. He walked over to the shelves against the back wall, farthest from the stairs, and found an assortment of small to medium boxes and a number of books. Three shoe boxes were labeled *Letters*. Two more were labeled *Family Records*, and two boot boxes were labeled *Photographs*. He couldn't remember seeing these boxes in his childhood.

Clarence selected one of the boxes labeled *Letters*, and blew and brushed off the accumulated dust. He pulled at the bow knot in the string that held the top on, and reached inside. The envelopes were dark with age, almost brown around the edges, splitting along the brittle corners. They didn't seem to be in any particular order. Several bore the address he knew so well from his childhood: Mr. and Mrs. Claude R. Harris, 25 Hoover St., Elliston, Georgia.

Some were addressed to Mrs. Ophelia Harris. He opened and unfolded one of them. It was from Mr. Hayden Carpenter, Culloden Orphan's Home, Birmingham, Alabama.

> Dear Mr. and Mrs. Harris,
>
> Thank you for your inquiry about adoption, and your visit of March 15, 1950. It was my pleasure to visit with you. You seem to be an ideal family for the placement of a child. However, because of the many requests we have had in the last few years, we are unable to give any encouragement about the possibility of adoption at this time. You will remain on our list, but because of the large number of waiting couples I cannot offer you any realistic hope for several years. I wish you success in your efforts to find a child elsewhere.
>
> Sincerely yours,
> H. Carpenter, Manager

Clarence frowned. He'd never heard his parents mention adoption. Had they been trying to get a brother or sister for him? No, not in 1950. Why would they be contacting an adoption agency the year he was born?

He kept tight hold of the letter as his gaze flicked unwillingly around the dusty attic in panic. He had to tell himself to stay calm. What other surprises would he find here today? These letters from the past contrasted oddly with his life today. It had almost been a different world back then. Now, he thought to himself, he had what was probably a fairly typical suburban lifestyle. He and Susan were well-dressed and enjoyed reliable transportation, good food, good medicine and pleasant neighbors. Three groups provided their social support and contentment: faculty and their spouses from the university, friends from their church, and of course their neighbors. These groups overlapped and both he and Susan had other close friends in civic and charitable groups.

Susan. How fortunate he had been to meet her. A woman beyond price, and both of them could almost be described as pillars of respectability, busy with life. Susan was deeply involved with their local church, amongst many other things helping out with Meals on Wheels, and he helped coach Little League baseball in the summers and the youth basketball team at the church. His need to help out with these youth programs had lessened in the years after his son Ed graduated from high school and moved away from home. So Clarence gave up coaching, although he kept up his interest in the school and church teams.

He thought of the way things had been sometimes difficult financially as a child, and now he had a good living as a professor at Clawson University in the mid-sized town of Clayton. It was a small university that started out as a Presbyterian college, but became an independent as church support became less fashionable and inadequate, and kept up its educational programs with endowments, strong alumni support and higher than average tuition. From the start it had been a liberal arts school, emphasizing religion and theology, although featuring a more general curriculum now.

Clarence smiled to himself. He loved the challenge of teaching biology. He taught five courses ranging from freshmen to graduate level and advised three students in their new Master of Science degree. He considered his comfortable life a fortunate one, and his love of his work was a major reason for this. It was certainly a long way from life in this country town where he grew up.

This tiny town of Elliston with about 400 people was 150 miles southeast of Clayton. His family had lived on what was then a sand-and-clay street in this, the house his grandfather built: sturdy, wood-framed, roofed with metal that drummed in the rain. The timbers of the house came from lumber sawed by Millard Harris, his grandfather. Millard Harris was a successful timber man who had supplied the timber that most of the houses in Elliston were built from. He was successful enough that he was able to build himself a much finer brick home on the other side of town where the few wealthier people lived.

Clarence's dad, Ruston Harris, and his young family had moved into the old family home in 1954, after Millard Harris moved out. Clarence was nearly four years old at the time. Although Ruston Harris earned a comfortable living as a brick mason, he never felt the need to move out of the sturdy wood frame house he grew up in. Clarence's mom and dad had a happy but unexciting life — at least he thought so now, looking back. His mother was active in the Wildwood Methodist Church over on Pulaski Street, and regularly visited many of the ladies in town; some in her church, some not. She made sure Clarence was in church every Sunday, dressed as fine as any of the other children.

His dad, Ruston, could never be accused of being a regular at church. He only showed up for weddings and funerals of relatives and close friends. In fact, his dad could be called anti-social. If it was not for this, Clarence realized now, perhaps for the first time, his parents would probably have been more prominent in the community. It was not a meanness of spirit that kept his father semi-isolated from the community, but a shy, withdrawn personality. Clarence had come to know that his dad was not as involved in the community as many of the other men in town. He never attached much importance to it or held it against him. He rather loved and respected his father, even though their bond had never been emotional.

His father Ruston had died fifteen years ago, and now his mother was almost certain to follow him within weeks, if not days.

Clarence's thoughts returned to the letter in his hand. Adoption? What was all that about? "Let's see," he calculated aloud, "it was written seven months before I was born. Surely Mama would have known she was pregnant after two months. But maybe not, not in those days of almost no pre-natal care." Had his parents been trying for a child for years, only to have one seven months after contacting the agency?

"So that's why I have no brothers or sisters," he thought, gripping the letter tightly, afraid to let it go, and equally afraid to keep hold of it. "They must have been so nearly infertile that I was the result of the only pregnancy they could muster."

Well, he had no complaints about that. Childhood was idyllic as he now looked back on it. He could remember no real problems. Well, there were the small ones caused by his shyness: bullies at school, girls who liked him at an age when he despised them, and chores around the house when he would rather be reading or roaming the nearby woods. His happiest times were in the woods, or in books of nature, adventure, and animals. His favorite characters came back from books and television in times of nostalgia: Huckleberry Finn, Tarzan, White Fang.

Clarence was lost in thought, taken back to a time when he played here with his boyhood pal Jeremy Bronson. This attic had been one of their favorite hideaways. He remembered the mystery of all the old items stored in this large, nearly empty space between the rooms and roof of this house where he learned about life. And here still were the same boxes, old toys and items that the family stopped using but couldn't bring themselves to throw away. But it seemed somehow much smaller now, no longer holding the fascination and excitement of the secret place it had been then.

Apart from this letter.

Something kept telling him that this letter he gripped so forcefully contained appalling news – if he could only look at it more closely. And this he couldn't bring himself to do. Not yet.

Instead, he let his attention turn to a wooden home-made rocking horse that he barely remembered. It was likely made by his father and painted by his mother. On a shelf on the far right was a baseball glove, dark with age, hard as wood and surely much smaller now than it had been once. A quart Mason jar half full of marbles reminded him of the game of roley-holey he and Jeremy used to play in the shade of a giant elm, in the hard dirt yard behind the house. He would steal one of Mama's table spoons to dig the small peach-sized holes laid out in a large L-shaped course. The holes were about three feet apart, and the starting line was at the top of the L. The first one to shoot his marble into all of the holes, down and back, won. You made the game tougher by hitting the opponent's marble with your own to knock it further away from the course.

He and Jeremy often came to the attic by way of the old oak that grew close to the roof over the back porch. They would climb the tree, shimmy out on the big limb, drop onto the porch roof and raise the small window into the attic. It wasn't the easiest way to get here. They could easily have gone up the stairs inside just off the bedrooms. But climbing was much more fun.

They told each other their most outrageous imaginations and recent experiences. Clarence learned much of what he knew at the time, or thought he knew, about sex and socialization from Jeremy. Jeremy had three older brothers and two sisters who brought a world of information home to him. Clarence was an only child. From eight to fifteen, Jeremy was his closest friend and constant buddy. In high school they grew apart because they played different sports, but mostly because Jeremy's family moved to a bigger, better house out of town.

He hadn't seen Jeremy since his second year in college. He heard from some of his mother's neighbors that Jeremy had moved to California and was driving a truck for a transport company. Just now, Clarence had a nostalgic longing for those days with Jeremy. He remembered, as happened so many times when he and Jeremy were playing, Mama calling at dusk from the kitchen door.

What would life have been like with other children in this house? His life, which had seemed so settled, might have been very different. What if his parents had been more fertile? How many siblings might he have? Maybe they were completely infertile! Maybe I was adopted!

Clarence was taken aback by these questions. They came flooding from some place in his mind he didn't even know existed until now. Where were the answers, the clues?

"If I was adopted, I would certainly know from something," he told himself firmly, but not very convincingly. "I would have seen it in family records, photographs, somewhere." He tried to visualize his birth certificate. Was there a clue, an error there? His mind was so stirred he couldn't remember his birth certificate, didn't know where it was, wasn't even sure he had one.

"I could ask Mama," he thought. Oh, but no, his mother was beyond asking now. "Maybe in a few weeks she'll recover enough to talk." Who was still around that might know? The old neighbors? Or Uncle Zack, Daddy's brother. Would he know? Mama's brother, Uncle Ted? Aunt Anne, Mama's unmarried sister? Dr. Clinton, who delivered me? Maybe not. Still, he *might* know!

Squatting in the gloom and dust of this attic, surrounded by his own and his parents' past, he felt uncomfortable. Strangely uncomfortable. Something unpleasant was right here in one of these boxes. The feeling wouldn't go away. One letter read, and a surprising secret from his past was slowly but surely being revealed. And however much he wanted to get up and run down those narrow stairs to the comfort and security of the rooms he knew so well, he felt compelled to remain. These boxes held something more significant, more life changing, than the papers he needed to take care of Mama's affairs.

Suddenly he stood up, his thoughts becoming more reasoned. Instead of coping with the poor light and uncomfortable squatting to read through the papers up here, he gathered up the boxes of letters and family records and headed downstairs.

He went to the dining-room table, set them down, and

went to look for something to drink. He returned with a can of Pepsi from the refrigerator and started sorting through the boxes. Most of the letters were from relatives who lived some distance from Elliston, mixed with bills presumably paid decades ago, bank statements from the 1950s through the 1970s, and photographs, some in envelopes, some loose.

He found photographs he had surely never seen. "Where were these boxes in the attic when I lived here?" he wondered. He had never seen them before. Well, maybe he had looked at them once, and never thought about them or their contents. No, he would surely have gone through them if they'd been here when he and Jeremy were spending so many hours up here with nothing better to do than explore.

He noticed, almost with horror, that he still clutched the letter from the adoption agency. He put it down reluctantly and started to rummage apprehensively through these boxes for something related. After going through the first box, Clarence realized he needed something to key on. The date! Nineteen-fifty was on the letter from the agency. He could narrow the search by date. He went back through the first box looking for 1950 on the envelopes and letterheads. No luck. Then he realized that 1951 might be a better year. The letter was dated March, 1950 and was a rejection. Perhaps his parents were continuing to look in 1951.

In the third box was a letter postmarked January 19, 1951, addressed to Mrs. Ophelia Harris, 25 Hoover St., Elliston, Ga.; with the return address Anne Harris, 120 Silver Streak Lane,

Birmingham, Ala.

"Aunt Anne, in Birmingham?" Clarence muttered. "That's where this came from." He slipped the single sheet out of the yellowed envelope and read a letter to his mother:

> Dear Ofie,
>
> You are in my prayers every day. I don't know what I did to deserve a lovely sister like you. I hope I can someday repay the debt I have against me for your kindness. You have rescued me from an impossible mistake.
>
> I should have never looked twice at Bill Timmons. I knew he was trouble, but to me he was irresistible. He was kind, romantic and fun to be with. God help me, I still love him. But I should have known he wouldn't stick with me. I found out he got another girl in trouble two years ago.
>
> I know my life will never be the same, but I have to go on. I will pray every day for you and Ruston and Clarence. I feel awfully unlucky for me, but really glad for Clarence. He is the luckiest of all, because he will always have you.
>
> Thank you for saving me. I will be his "Aunt" by whatever rules you set.
>
> All my love, Anne.

Clarence felt shaken for the second time in an hour. He laid his head down on his arms on the table and closed his eyes. Unbelievable! He tried not to think, tried to relax, tried to calm down. But a hundred questions tumbled out of his brain. Did the letter really mean what it seemed to? Did the letter from the adoption agency mean that his mother was barren? *Was he really his aunt's son?* Aunt Anne was the most distant of his aunts and uncles, and she always seemed unfriendly and aloof at family reunions. He recalled how she always spoke to him in a strained voice, and seemed to care nothing for him. Surely Aunt Anne was not his mother.

He had never an inkling of it before, but now he remembered the hurt look in her countenance. Unusual glances that a kid would notice but not understand. And she was never around. Well, maybe once or twice a year. Could this be the reason? Was it the pain of being unable to love her own son? Clarence didn't know whether to hate or pity her. His mother, a "distant" relative! He had been a lifetime in the dark about his beginning.

Now he was torn with conflict. Should he confront his mother with the secret, and let her know the indignation he felt? Should he blame his biological mother for abandoning him? Should he blame his adopted mother, his real mother, for not telling? Surely it was her place to tell him. But tell him what – that his aunt was his mother!

Maybe it was all a mistake. Maybe the letter was a fraud, a prank. He didn't want to believe it. Old secrets like this might not be what they seem at first. After he confronted the people still around who would know, the reality might be quite different. But did he really want to know? Until now he had been completely comfortable with his life history — yes, until now. What would be accomplished by confronting relatives with a secret they were willing to keep; had kept for over fifty years?

Clarence stood up, feeling the need to get out of the house and walk. Maybe that would help settle him down, clear his mind. He walked out of his boyhood home, into the street that had once been dirt, and headed west toward the edge of town, away from the north-south highway that was the Main Street of Elliston.

Three blocks west, fields and forest began when he was a boy. Now he saw a new subdivision where he used to climb trees and wade in the small stream. Some of the old trees had been saved, but the terrain was unrecognizable. He and Jeremy had built a tree house in a large oak somewhere in this subdivision, in a grove of trees that made it invisible from more than twenty-five yards. There was no clue now where it might have been.

As he stood staring at the subdivision, but seeing nothing, Clarence suddenly realized he needed to call Susan. He needed to tell her his discovery. At least she would know the sensible thing to do. Steady Susan! She had always been his best source of advice, his safe way out of controversy and stress. Now he needed to tell her what he had learned, and get her advice about what to do.

He headed back to the house. At the kitchen telephone he dialed Susan. She answered right away. "Hello, sweetheart. I'm calling to tell you some devastating news I learned... No, it's not about Mama, she's fine... No, I mean she's about the same. Still no response." Clarence tried to use his normal voice, but he guessed Susan could tell that he was stressed to distraction, not making much sense.

"Are you at the nursing home?" she asked.

"No, I'm at Mama's house. I've been going through some old records. You won't believe what I found."

"What is it, Clarence? Is it bad?"

He should have realized his wife would be able to read much into his voice. "No. Uh... I don't know. Can you come down here?" He didn't mean to ask that, but the question asked itself. He needed to talk, and she was coming in a couple of days anyway.

"You know I have to help with that garage sale at the church tomorrow. What is it that's so urgent?"

"It's not urgent, Susan. I, uh... found some letters in Mama's attic today. They say I was adopted. I never heard anything about it before. I don't know what to make of it. I wish we could talk."

"You must be kidding!" Susan sounded as though she knew he wasn't kidding. "I'm really sorry, Clarence. I don't know what to say. How do you feel?"

"Confused."

Susan seemed to be waiting for him to say something more, but he kept silent. "Do you really think it's true?" she asked at last. "What did the letters say?"

"I need to talk to you, but not on the phone." In that moment Clarence made up his mind to go back to Clayton. He could get there by dark if he left now. "Susan, I'm coming home this afternoon."

"But what about your mother?"

"It won't make any difference to her if I'm here or not. She doesn't even know when I'm in the room."

"We could go down together tomorrow as soon as I'm finished at the church," Susan promised. "You can help us get ready for the sale."

"I'd like to." And with that, Clarence said goodbye, gathered up the boxes of letters and prepared to leave.

On the three-hour drive back to Clayton he tried to sort out the facts and feelings of the last few weeks. He had lost, for practical purposes, the person who had once meant the most to his life. Now he'd learned that he didn't belong to her in the beginning, but was a borrowed child. Did it make any difference? Apparently Mama and Daddy wanted a child. They had applied for adoption. So how did they feel about adopting Mama's sister's illegitimate child? Perhaps Mama would recover enough to explain. If she did, would he find out how she felt? Would he have the courage, would he have the disrespect, to bring it up?

Aunt Anne was now a suddenly central figure in his

thoughts, not the distant relative he'd known. Had she really wanted to give him up? What was his biological father like? Was he still living? What did Aunt Anne mean to him anyway? What had she meant to Mama after this sacrifice? Who had made the greater sacrifice? What was he to do now? Follow the old comfortable road, or explore this new one to the unknown? He could walk away from this new discovery, pretend it was still hidden. He could burn the letters and any others he might find. Or could he?

Was there a stigma attached to adoption? Surely it was a common enough event in some families. But your *aunt's* child? What could he tell his two children, Ed and Erin? Would they even begin to understand, or would it rip the family apart? And his grandchildren, Christine and Catherine. Would they have to be told one day that their great grandmother was not really who everyone had thought she was? And his church? Supposing everyone there found out? He already resented all of the questions and sympathy that would follow.

It seemed to come down to deceit. His own parents had deceived him, leading him to believe they were his real mother and father, and in turn he had deceived his wife, his children, his grandchildren, although in innocence, over the identity of his folks.

"Lord God," he prayed, "help me through this mess. Help Susan and all my family through this mess too."

Until now his faith had provided all the comfort and security he needed to live as a committed Christian. Would God steer him through this time of uncertainty, of not knowing where he belonged?

* * *

At home, Susan opened the door to him. They embraced for several minutes without speaking. Finally, Susan said, "Let's go in the den and talk. I want to know about your mother."

Clarence crashed down in a chair and sighed. "I honestly can't say she's changed since we were there last week. I tried to talk, but I don't think she even hears me."

He wanted to change the subject. Wanted to talk about his devastating discovery. "There's much more to it than that," he said at last, taking the two letters out of his pocket. "I wish I could have found these at some other time. You'd better read them." He stood and handed Susan the one from the adoption agency.

She read slowly, then looked up. "It only shows that your parents were interested in adoption."

He passed her the other letter without saying anything. After reading, Susan stood and hugged him again, the letter still in her hand. "I'm so sorry, Clarence. I can see why you're confused. What do you want to do?"

He shook his head. He felt in a daze. "I honestly don't know. Maybe I want to burn them. Can we talk about this later?"

"But you came home specially to talk about it now."

"If I burn these letters, we won't need to talk about it, ever, will we?" he said in a hopeful voice. He'd hurried home to get

Susan's advice and solace. Now he wished he hadn't bothered. He wanted to leave it alone, wanted to be rid of the uncertainty and conflict he saw ahead on this unknown road of discovery.

Susan gave him another hug. "It won't erase anything, Clarence. You'll always know what you have learned today. There may be more to this, or there may be something you'll be glad you found out. It's not like you to turn away from the truth, no matter how unpleasant. You won't find anything that makes you feel less of a person or that makes me love you less. You may find out that someone, your aunt, your mother, or your father did something you wouldn't approve of. But I don't think it will diminish them for you."

"And then what do I do?" he asked.

"Do? You're not a judgmental person, Clarence. You may find that someone made a great sacrifice for you. You may be a better man because of that sacrifice. You may have a chance to thank them, or at least tell them you understand. In the end this discovery can't hurt if you're the forgiving person I know."

"Well, at least I know where you stand," Clarence said. He usually accepted Susan's view without question, but on this he was not sure. "Anyway, I don't feel like talking about it now. I really am tired. Let's talk about it later."

"Sure," she said. "Why not wait until your mother is better, then bring it up? She might even help you handle it."

"If she wanted to help me with it, she had all my life to do it," he said abruptly, with a trace of bitterness that surprised him. "I'm sorry, I really don't want to talk about it."

* * *

His mother passed away the next day. Susan took the call about an hour after they had finished with the garage sale and were preparing for the trip to Elliston. She broke the news to Clarence by reaching for him as he opened the door to rush in from packing the car. She didn't say anything; he saw it in her eyes, in the drawn and startled look of her face. He had almost guessed it when he heard the phone ring. Even though it was not unexpected, he felt as if he had suddenly lost part of his life. He certainly didn't feel like going to Elliston and making arrangements for a funeral.

The next three days were the worst of his life, but they made him more thankful than ever that he had married Susan. He didn't feel grateful, though, until later, after the grief subsided. She was so steady, so levelheaded. She took over the arrangements.

When he felt like he couldn't go on, she put her arms around him and said, "Clarence, you don't know how proud your mother was of you. Once, when we were alone, she told me you were her greatest success."

Clarence shook his head, wondering what he had done to deserve a wonderful wife like this, to support and encourage him when life became almost unbearable.

Five days later, when the funeral was over, and he and Susan were returning home, he agreed to take a week off from the university and go to Joe and Tracy Lunsford's cabin in the mountains. The Lunsfords, good friends in the same neighborhood, had offered them the cabin several times, and they had never had a chance to use it. And now seemed like a good time.

So on Monday morning they packed the rest of the clothes, the food and the gear they would need, and set off for the cabin. It was a three-hour drive due north, most of it on mountainous roads. Clarence had packed his fishing tackle and some of his bird-watching gear. Bird study was not only his research specialty at the university, it was his passion. He was sure he could relieve some of the grief and stress with several days outdoors. Susan would fish some with him, but spend much of her time reading.

Monday afternoon they spent unpacking, sweeping out the cabin, going three miles into the small village of Thompson to get food for the refrigerator, and some beer and soft drinks.

Early on Tuesday Clarence loaded his fishing tackle into the car and went to Lake Kimble for a few hours of fishing. He bought a bucket of minnows to use for bait, rented a boat for half a day and got out on the lake just after sunup. He felt better than he had in the weeks since his mother had suffered her stroke. The crisp air, clear sky, and fresh, wide vista on the lake surrounded by beautiful green forest rejuvenated him. His mind was further eased by a large red-tailed hawk he saw circling above the trees just back from the edge of the lake.

Clarence had been a birdwatcher all his life. His fondest memories from childhood were lying or sitting quietly in the fields and woods simply watching birds, studying and memorizing their individual behavior patterns. Hawks and vultures gliding effortlessly across the sky charmed him. Purple martins at Grandpa Harris' house flitting about the gourds hanging from a high pole in the backyard entertained him for hours. Brown thrashers scratching among the leaves and twigs for worms and bugs in that briar patch just down the street behind Old Man Steven's house were just as entertaining. He was surprised, even as a boy, at the vast number of varieties and sizes of birds, the array of habitats they used, and the many different ways they sang, nested and foraged for food.

He felt lucky to do for a living what he enjoyed most as a boy. As a professor at Clawson University he taught courses in biology dealing with most of the basic topics, but his research and main interest was connected with birds. He specialized in the study of hawks, those birds of prey that birdwatchers are ambivalent about and farmers hated, especially farmers who had baby chickens outside.

He thought often about the controversy that he heard in his childhood about the damage and benefits of birds of prey. Grandpa Harris was adamant that hawks were the worst pest he had to fight in raising baby chicks. He even accused them of scaring off and killing martins that he encouraged to nest in his gourds.

Clarence had landed two mid-sized bream by the middle of the morning, when he saw a man appear on the bank with a rod and reel to do some casting into the lake. With him was a small boy, apparently not yet old enough to be in school. Clarence stood watching with interest. The man was hampered in fishing because of the boy's interests in all things along the bank, especially in the water. After pulling him back from the water's edge several times, the father gave up on casting and sat down, back away from the water, with the boy playing around him.

Clarence sighed. The sight of the father and son brought back his puzzle about adoption. All the questions came back in a rush. How old was he when adopted? According to Aunt Anne's letter he must have been less than a year. He wondered if his father had fished with him at a young age like this father. His father was never as close as some fathers were to their sons. He never remembered his father taking him fishing until he was a teenager. He didn't remember the rough-housing, tumbling, and wrestling this father and son were now enjoying.

He knew, though, that Ruston Harris had been a good father. He had fond memories of traveling and working together. Clarence helped regularly in his teenage years with masonry jobs his father contracted. They went on fishing trips and hunted small game together around Elliston. His father treated him more like a companion than a son, except on those occasions when he needed correction or encouragement. Ruston Harris had been reticent on both counts. Clarence smiled wryly. It was his mother who had taken care of most of the discipline and support.

He wondered how his father felt about raising his sister-in-law's son. He obviously went along with it, but surely it was his mother who agreed to it, instigated it and relished it. Would his father have treated him differently if he had been his biological son? It was an unanswerable, unfathomable question. A waste of time.

And so his thoughts turned to Aunt Anne, the main character in the story that was usurping his mind. What was she to him? It too, was a troubling question, although one he could still do something about. But could he get the answers he wanted or needed? Could he enlighten his past and smooth his future by searching for answers, or would he make it worse? Susan was right: he could never erase what he had learned, and it was likely he could learn a lot more if he pursued it. But was the understanding he might find worth the chance that it would cost him the wonderful, peaceful world that existed before his mother's stroke?

There was also the chance that he might open old sores without getting answers. Why would Aunt Anne even agree to talk about his dilemma? She might even deny it. What had she to gain? And where would he be with his questions — accusations, even — standing there against her incredulous denials. He would look and feel foolish and remorseful if she convinced him she knew nothing about his adoption. She could even claim she knew nothing about a letter. Clarence dreaded to face her. She had hugged him at the funeral, but apart from that he had avoided her, perhaps more out of distraction by his sorrow than evasion.

So, what to do? One sure thing not to do today — fishing. He desperately wanted to relax and forget, but he could not. So, he put away his fishing gear and headed back to the cabin.

Susan sounded surprised when the cabin door slammed. "You're back early," she yelled from the screened-in back porch.

"No, I lost interest," Clarence said, halfway through the kitchen. He stopped at the sink and drew a glass of water from the tap and walked out onto the porch where Susan was reading the latest John Grisham book.

"I hope you caught enough for dinner," she said with a smile.

He drank half of the glass before saying anything. Then, "I went fishing to relax and forget, but it didn't work." He flopped down on the wicker couch next to Susan. "I can't get that letter off my mind. Maybe I should talk to Aunt Anne."

Susan took his left hand in both of hers. "Do you think you're ready? Do you think *she's* ready?"

"I don't know." He shook his head. "I have a few days on my hands, unless I go back to work. Maybe that's what I ought to do, just go to work and try to get back into my routine."

"Not if you're just going to sit at your desk and think of nothing else but this problem. You can probably think better here, or at home working in the garden."

"Maybe." He looked up. "Maybe it's not too early to talk to Aunt Anne. I think I'd feel a lot better if I could get some answers from her."

Susan kept hold of his hand. "It's chancy. You have a load of emotion right now. A confrontation with your aunt could make it worse."

He said nothing.

"You've got that faraway look in your eye," she said. "I can tell by the set of your jaw that you've already made up your mind. All right, perhaps a visit to Aunt Anne would get you back to normal sooner. How long would it take to drive to her house?"

He felt a sudden shock of surprise, but an unexpected feeling of relief flooded through him. "It's been so long, I really don't know. I'm sure she still lives in Dryden. We couldn't go without calling first. She might be out, or away."

"I don't think *we* ought to go at all. I think *you* ought to go. What would I contribute? She might tell you something she doesn't want anyone else to know."

"No, Susan, I want you with me."

She gave a little laugh. "You just want me along to lessen your fear, and to have someone to lean on. I think it's best kept as a meeting just for two."

Clarence felt uneasy. "How can I make sure I say the right things?"

"Just be straight. Tell her you found the letter and that you'd like to know about your origin. Don't ask her why you were never told. Don't try to blame anybody for anything. Ask as few questions as needed. Just listen, even if Aunt Anne wants to fill in with unnecessary details. Let her do it her way. It may be harder for her than for you."

He laughed, relaxing slightly. "You're sounding like a school teacher. Should I take along a recorder?"

"Do you have one?"

"Not with me. Should I take notes?"

"No."

"Do you want to stay here in the cabin, or go back home to Clayton?"

Susan shrugged. "Why don't we both go home? You can leave from there, and I can do some things I need to do about the house." She bit her lip. "Wait a minute, you may need to be away from work more than ever after you talk to Aunt Anne. Maybe I should stay here."

That sounded sensible. "If I leave right away I should be able to get back tonight."

He called information to get Anne Harris' number in Dryden and dialed it. When she answered, Clarence asked if he could come by and talk about his mother. Aunt Anne seemed pleased to receive his call and maybe even anxious to see him. There seemed to be no hint that she suspected his motive.

On the way to Dryden Clarence played over the questions he had gone over so many times before. How or even when should he bring up the subject of his adoption? He mustn't appear angry about how he'd been treated, but he couldn't appear unconcerned either. Should he show her the letter? No, simplicity was the best approach. He would just tell her in a matter of fact way what he had found, and then let her talk.

The first houses of Dryden came into sight at last. The encounter just a few minutes ahead could be disappointing, but on the other hand it could make him very happy. Yes, he expected revelations about his early life, and the loss of his mother had taken a heavy toll. Now he could be further devastated — or maybe unburdened by good news. The uncertainty heightened his anticipation.

R Harold Brown

Reconciliation

Anne Harris lived on a shady country lane on the far edge of the small town of Dryden. The town seemed similar in size and appearance to Elliston. There were two service stations. One appeared as it must have been built in the mid twentieth century with old tires stacked on the side, and two pumps with half the paint off, the words barely visible. The other was a modern convenience store with too many lights and too many signs advertising too many products on the plate glass windows. Clarence drove down the main street past the service stations, two empty stores, a rustic *Barbeque Shack* with only enough room for a couple of tables, and the unkempt post office that looked as if it had once doubled as a store.

Just beyond the post office he turned left onto Church Street and passed both the Dryden United Methodist and Dryden Baptist churches. Then Eunice Lane angled to the right and down a slight hill past several small wood frame houses. At the end was the larger white house that Aunt Anne had described.

It was an early 1900s house, probably built by a prosperous merchant. The secondary story was about half the size as the first floor. The green metal roof descended steeply on all four sides, with large dormers providing daylight for the second story. A walk made of bricks, bordered with daffodils, ran from the entrance gate to the front steps. Time had made the walk rough by shifting bricks up or down, but it was still attractive.

Clarence pulled up parallel to the gate in the white picket fence and sat in the car for a couple of minutes. The sizeable yard had several large trees and a rough lawn in places where there was not too much shade. Azalea bushes seemed to grow everywhere.

"It must be a beautiful place in early spring," he decided as he got out of the car into the hot afternoon air and walked over to the white gate to let himself in. As he reached for the latch, he heard the opening of the front door and squeaking of hinges of the screen door. His aunt, half hidden in the doorway, was coming to see who had arrived.

To his surprise, she was dressed just like his mother used to dress, with a bright white and yellow flowered print skirt and a solid yellow blouse. Clarence stared. She looked so much like his mother from that distance that he hesitated to open the gate. The fears he had about this encounter flooded back. How could he bring up the subject he felt so awkward about?

As he walked up the brick walk, Aunt Anne walked to the edge of the large porch and stood on the top step. He quickened his pace and reached the bottom of the steps before speaking. "Hey, Aunt Anne, how are you?"

"Clarence! It's so good to see you."

"I'm sorry I didn't get... to see you... to talk long at the funeral," he said awkwardly, with no idea what to do or say next. At the top of the steps he took her hand, but he was speechless. In all his life, before crowds, in conferences, in embarrassing moments, he couldn't remember a more incompetent feeling. "Aunt Anne," he finally blurted in a faltering voice, "I don't know what to say."

She squeezed his hand. "How about something to drink? I have some tea made, and I just baked some cookies. Would you like some?"

He found himself wondering if she suspected anything about his visit. "Sure."

"We'll go through the kitchen and sit on the back porch."

As they went through a hallway paneled with narrow tongue-and-grooved pine boards that needed repainting, Aunt Anne turned to ask, "How is Susan?"

He thought of lying about how Susan wanted to come but couldn't. "She's fine."

In the kitchen Aunt Anne filled two glasses with ice, and then poured tea. She asked him to take the glasses to the porch, and she followed with the platter of cookies. Clarence looked out through the screen of the porch and saw the back yard was covered with shrubbery: azaleas, rhododendron, crape myrtle, holly near the porch and several dogwoods among the large oaks. He saw two cardinals and a bossy blue jay contesting for food at a bird feeder hanging in a dogwood.

About thirty feet from the porch steps was an old well with

a brick curb and a wooden covering like so many he saw while growing up. The bucket and the rope and tackle were missing, along with the scaffold that held the tackle. It was a sign that although wells remain, the manual drawing of water was history. It was also a sign of the progress of his mother's generation from laborious living to modern convenience. He wondered if Aunt Anne's water came from a pump in that well, or from the town.

He sat at one end of a long primitive wooden bench made comfortable with bright colored home-made cushions. They were tied securely in place with ribbon-strings made of the same material. Aunt Anne sat near Clarence toward the center of the bench. He wasn't quite ready to ask the hard question, so he made small talk. "You have quite a bird haven out here. Do you like to watch birds?"

Aunt Anne gave a small laugh. "No, not much. I feed them often, but don't spend much time watching. I can't really tell one kind from another. I'm afraid I couldn't even talk birds with an expert like you."

He was surprised again how much she looked like his mother when she smiled about declining to talk birds with an expert. Her eyes brightened and the eyebrows rose slightly. He was also surprised that she knew he was a bird expert. But, why shouldn't she? His mother had probably told her many times.

There was a lull that seemed like minutes. He recognized it as the kind of pause that characterizes discussion between people with little in common. Well, he thought, it's now or never.

"Aunt Anne, I came here today to ask you some questions. I hope you don't mind."

She looked almost amused. "Of course not."

"Am I adopted?"

Anne's bright eyes had been looking straight at his face, and this question caused the brightness to fade as quickly as if a switch had been thrown. Her eyes fell and looked away across the yard. After a few seconds she said simply, "Yes."

He detected a note of resignation in her voice that told him that what he had learned was true, that she had not expected to be asked, and that she had now given up the life-long secret. So many questions he'd had on his drive over. Now he didn't know what to ask next.

When Aunt Anne looked back at him, he could see tears had formed, and the hurt he'd seen moments ago had intensified. "Why did you ask?" she said in a whisper. "I mean, how did you know?"

"I found this in Mama's attic." He handed his aunt the letter.

She took it and put it in her lap. She looked at Clarence through her tears, and after blinking a few times, stood and said, "I am so sorry, Clarence. You've been hurt badly recently, and I'm so sorry you've suffered this second hurt."

Her emotions overcame her and she broke down completely, sobbing and wiping at her eyes with the napkin she'd been holding around the glass of tea.

She started to walk back toward the kitchen and Clarence jumped up and took her in his arms. Her sobbing got louder. He started crying, and tried to talk to her at the same time. "It's okay, Aunt Anne. It's not your fault. I'm okay. I don't blame you for anything."

She regained some of her composure. "I always knew you'd find out someday. I'm sorry it happened this way. I didn't know what to do then; I don't know what to do now. Forgive me, Clarence." She broke into sobs again.

Clarence didn't talk, couldn't talk. He just held on.

His Aunt pulled away, dabbing her eyes and not looking at him, "Clarence, give me a few minutes. I'll tell you what I can."

With that she walked away through the kitchen, unsteady on her feet. Clarence sat down, feeling numb. He was barely aware of Aunt Anne's return. She had a large scrapbook in her arms, a black loose-leaf type, worn through the black coating at the edges from frequent use, giving it a thin border of gray. She sat down, but made no motion to open it. "This is a detailed scrapbook of your life, Clarence. I kept up with you all the time as you were growing up. You must have read about my interest in you from all the letters I wrote to Ofie."

Suddenly he realized that he had never even looked at all the letters at his mother's house. They might have answered many of the questions he had asked in his anxiety. He silently cursed his habit of jumping to conclusions without examining all the possibilities. He knew he was much worse at it than most people. "I found that one first and didn't look further."

He stood to leave. Further questions seemed unimportant now. "Aunt Anne, you have been so understanding and kind. I'm really glad I came this afternoon."

"Clarence!" she cut him off. "It is *I* who have been blessed by your coming. You don't know how much it means to me. I've been so sorry for so many years about the biggest mistake of my life, but I don't see it that way now. I don't know what to call it, how to feel about it. If it wasn't for that mistake you wouldn't have been born."

The result of a mistake? Clarence felt thunderstruck. What a beginning! He grasped for the first time the blessing of that "mistake". Life! His greatest gift, his being, the result of a young girl's lapse! There were no negatives in this "mistake".

He left Aunt Anne's house with a high spirit, with all the grief of the last few weeks lifted. All those unanswered questions were unimportant. Perhaps he would sift through them again in the coming days and need answers, but for now his mind was full of the enormous answer he had just received. His happy life, his very being, was given to him by this woman he had just come to know. What a debt! What a joyous debt!

Oh, woman! A sister, a twin in spirit, to the mother who raised him. A sister in spirit to Susan his wife who told him a few days ago, "You may find that someone made a great sacrifice for you that you never suspected" How lucky to be surrounded by three of the most incredible women since Eve: his mother, Susan, and now Aunt Anne!

His step was lighter, his thoughts energetic, his overarching feeling one of gratitude. He felt as if he had a new life, as if he was born again. He, Clarence Harris, was the luckiest man alive.

And already he suspected he didn't know the half of it.

Not yet.

A Day at Work

Clarence felt lousy. It wasn't his work that had him down; in fact things at the university office were going okay. He hadn't slept well last night and was sluggish — not hurting, but not functioning very well. He was spending his time on problems other than the most pressing ones.

He went over again and again the astounding revelation of a couple of months ago, when he had learned that he was Aunt Anne's son. He had considered all of the angles and still came to the same conclusion — he was lucky to have become completely reconciled to his biological mother immediately after the revelation.

Incredibly, there were no recriminations on his part. He felt the terrible loss of his adopted mother and always would, but coming to know his aunt was indeed a blessing. She had visited several times in the last two months and had written several times. Susan and their children and grandchildren had accepted her with great love and affection. What a wonderful family! He certainly felt blessed.

Even before Aunt Anne had joined their family, their two

children brought them great joy and the usual anxiety. Twenty-seven years ago they had their first, a daughter named Erin Elizabeth. They both doted on Erin. Clarence was as eager to spend time with her as an infant and adolescent as he was with Ed who was born two years later. The whole family spent many weekends camping, fishing, and walking the woods. Clarence tried to transfer his love of nature and even of birds to the children, especially Ed, but it hadn't worked. Rock music, electronic games, and later, computers, turned out to be Ed's preoccupation and livelihood. He played in an amateur rock band as a teen. Though Clarence and Susan were wary of his teenage friends and his prospects for a proper career, Ed had become something of a computer expert and had a well-paying job. Their main lingering qualms were his limited social life and confirmed bachelorhood; and, of course, no grandchildren.

Erin, on the other hand, had twins, Christine and Catherine who were a delight for Clarence and Susan. They were most pleased when they could find the time to visit Erin and her husband, Tom, or entice them to come to Clayton to visit. Erin had been a good student, majored in science education, and had taught in middle school for three years before the twins were born. She was now a stay-at-home mom and as happy as Clarence could remember.

This morning, though, in his office at Clawson University it was mostly the mundane problems that occupied his mind. Susan's car was now in the shop. Herman had just called and given him the news — new tires all around. It didn't seem that long since he bought the last set.

It was always something in this rat-race: new tires this week, repair of the home furnace three weeks ago, and soon the roof would have to be replaced. So many things needed, and so little money left over at the end of the month. He was trying to save for the boat and motor he had wanted for so long. Not a large inboard boat and trailer that some of his friends and people from the office had — just an aluminum jon-boat and small motor. Actually, he and Susan were much better off financially now that the kids were out of college. They were simply trying to make sure that there would be enough for a comfortable and safe retirement.

Since about eleven this morning, he had felt tightness in his chest, like indigestion. Probably the hot sauce he splashed on his omelet this morning. Susan had prepared his favorite breakfast, an egg-cheese-pepper omelet with onions and southwestern seasoning. Half the time it gave him heartburn; this was probably one of those times. But he had felt this new sensation last night. Heartburn with a constriction, hours before breakfast. Oh well, there was no time to dwell on it now.

He was worrying about the talk he was to give at the state biology meeting beginning Thursday of next week on his research — hawk nesting habits. Bird biology was not only his job, but his very favorite daydream. Before planning for that conference he had to get past four more class lectures in Biology 101. He stewed about each one. Why did so many of his faculty friends always seem so nonchalant about preparing for class? Although he had taught this class many times in the fifteen years he had been at Clawson University, he fretted about each lecture.

It was certainly much easier now than the first few times, but he was worried that he was falling behind in some area of biology where he should be current. Although the class had a textbook to follow, he believed up-to-date examples made the class less drab. Drab? That was what he feared in his classes more than anything. Although student ratings were good and the department chairman was pleased with his performance, he couldn't allow himself to get complacent.

Today's lecture was about genetics, the second of several. To help fight boredom in his students, he used examples like blue eyes cropping up in brown-eyed families, and calico coat patterns showing up only in female cats. Students were fascinated to learn that genetics was discovered by a monk, Gregor Mendel, while he was studying the ratios of flower colors on pea plants, produced by cross-breeding plants with different flower colors. Mendel published his results in 1866, but the mechanics and mathematics that described behavior of chromosomes and genes could easily bore the students today.

The next lesson included the basics of reproduction, the joining of male and female cells to form embryos. The trick was to excite interest in learning about the process, without boring or losing the student. He knew that stimulation to learn was more important than getting the facts across. Nearly all of the facts were there in black and white in the book. Like all good teachers, he knew that mastering the art of stimulation contributed more to education than writing a book.

Speaking the students' language was important too, but introducing scientific expression was necessary so they could understand the text and read other sources in the future. New terms had to be introduced carefully and gradually.

He needed to keep excitement in his voice. He had to have the excitement in his mind, in his body, in his projection, in his demeanor. Not a hollow, contrived animation; he had to believe what he was saying made a difference in the education of the students. Every person was enriched by what he or she learned, and learning about the passing of traits from one generation to another was as important as any lesson. It was the core of creation. Yes, he realized, it was the renewal of life.

Clarence walked into class five minutes before starting time. He could see a few students lounging in the seats near the front of the room, reviewing the basketball team's problems. Most were blaming the coach. One couple was holding hands and nuzzling in the far left corner, oblivious of the others, including Clarence. When the students saw him, they forgot basketball and turned to see if the professor had any comments of the day. Except the loving couple. They didn't notice. During the inquiries about what the class would cover in the next week, when mid-term exams would be, and what kinds of questions to expect, more students drifted into the classroom.

At 1:15 Clarence walked to the podium, opened his notebook and announced that today's lecture would cover conception, birth and chromosome behavior in mammals, including humans.

"The miracle of birth has a scientific basis," he announced, "and the behavior of genes, chromosomes and reproductive cells determine who we are."

Using charts, photographs, and practiced, logical movement through the subject, he seemed to be keeping the attention of most of the students through the lecture.

They learned that plants and animals alike are conceived by the union of male and female gametes: sperm and egg cells. In immobile plants the pollen unites with the ovary in a mostly passive process. In mammals the male usually searches out the female, and in an active coupling the sperm fertilizes the egg. The pairing of chromosomes, one set from the male and one from the female, in that new cell or *zygote* brings together the genes from the parents that determine the looks and habits of the new being.

He told the class that there were exceptions that they would learn later, and gave the example that in some plants and animals, new individuals can be formed by parthenogenesis, without any genes from the male.

One of the strange things that always struck him when he gave this lecture was the overkill of male cells. Female cells were so far outnumbered as to make the mismatch obvious, if not astounding. He decided now to use the example of pollen in spring when trees are in bloom. Although oak trees can produce hundreds of acorns, each representing a fertilized egg cell, the number of pollen cells produced by most plants is astronomical. To illustrate, he showed a slide of the relative size of acorns and pollen grains. Although individual pollen grains are too small to see with the naked eye, they coat cars, sidewalks and houses in such large numbers as to make them yellow.

When Clarence called for questions at the end of the lecture, Ben Carter in the third row raised his hand.

"How many... uh... sperm does the man...? I mean, when..."

Clarence rescued Ben from the rest of the embarrassing question by anticipating, but he had no good answer. In fact, he had no idea. "It must be a tremendous number..." From somewhere deep inside he felt his brain disengage itself from the answer on his lips. "I don't know," he said at last. "Hundreds. Maybe thousands."

On The Bypass

Clarence knew something had happened that required an answer, not for Ben, but for himself. He couldn't dismiss class fast enough so he could head for his office. When he reached the desk, he saw the telephone answering machine blinking a waiting message. He pressed the button and heard Susan reminding him that he was due at the dentist's office in twenty minutes. Even if he left immediately he would barely have time to make the appointment. No time to organize the papers and books he needed to take home to work on his next lecture, or that speech for the Biology meeting next week.

    He wheeled his Jeep Wagon out of the parking lot too fast and headed for the bypass and the dentist's office on the other side of town. He glanced at his fuel gauge and realized he might run out of gas before he got there. So a couple of blocks before the bypass he pulled quickly into the "Pump Jump" convenience store to get enough to make sure. He pumped the gasoline and hurried inside to pay his five dollars even, so he wouldn't have to wait for change. He was impatient, but his impatience ramped up several notches when he saw the down-

and-out lottery player at the cash register.

The man was searching all of his pockets for coins and bills, sorting through the cigarettes, string, scraps of paper and other trash from his pockets, while at the same time trying to decide which game he should bet on. Clarence had noticed outside that the Grand Regional Lottery pot was up to eighty-seven million.

He disliked the lottery on principle. Why should the government fund public property and services by pandering to the craving of citizens for undeserved wealth? Sure, some urges in people should be cultivated by government, but not the spending of hard-earned money in the expectation of something for nothing. This man at the counter clearly couldn't afford the chance he was taking. He needed the money for other things: a haircut, for example, some new clothes, or at least a good cleaning of the ones he was wearing to help them last him a little longer.

"A tax on the stupid," he had once heard someone say. It fits, he thought, but stupidity wasn't the only flaw that caused purchase of lottery tickets. Even people who were smart enough to own fancy cars and nice homes spent money on the lottery, hoping to increase their wealth even further.

No matter, the deck was stacked against this homeless man. Clarence felt a little guilty that he already had fit the man in a "homeless" box after only a quick look at his clothes and manners.

Clarence frowned. Was this bum at the counter to blame

when he was constantly bombarded by advertisements, government sponsored expectations, and convenience stores that take his money even though his chances were near zero?

"My chances of making it to the dentist's office on time are also approaching zero, because of this stupid man wallowing in this stupid lottery," Clarence muttered angrily.

The man finished, gave him a scattered-tooth grin, and headed for the door, leaving a smell of the accumulated human residue of oils of the skin and grime of the street.

As he left the store and turned onto the ramp to the bypass, Clarence relaxed a little, and the looming speech on hawk nesting came into his mind. There was no problem deciding what to present. The data were collected and summarized some time ago, and it was now a matter of selecting the newest and most interesting observations. Only a few slides still needed to be made, maybe four or five. Organize it, polish it, practice a time or two – and he'd be ready.

In a couple of minutes he would be passing a grove of trees where a pair of red-tailed hawks had built a nest that he'd been watching for weeks. It wasn't a part of his work, but he was keenly interested. The nest was somewhere in the trees off to the right, and up the hill about a hundred meters. The baby birds should be just about ready to fly now. He made a mental note to come back and inspect the nest tomorrow, Saturday, or perhaps the next day.

He thought about how an animal, as far removed as hawks were from humans, could have similar habits. The red-tailed mated for life and settled into an area it never left unless disturbed or enticed away. Much like the hawk, Clarence was completely committed to Susan. Married for thirty-one years and not about to give up the best thing that had happened to him. They were also married to their community and their church, which supplied everything he and Susan needed. They both liked travel, but never as much as getting back to their home, friends and community.

Just beyond the tree with the hawk nest was a roadway beneath the bypass. Grovetown Road was in a small natural valley, and the bypass had bridged over it with a large span that sat high above the old road.

As Clarence passed the trees, his mind turned quickly to the question Ben Carter had asked about the number of sperm cells produced by a man at mating. He knew the answer was "many", and it would have been a sufficient answer once. But not now.

"Why have I not asked myself that question before," he said to himself. "And why am I even bringing it up now?" It was just one of millions of details in biology; no one can know them all. A large portion is not worth knowing, at least not worth memorizing. But all are important in some context where they fit and support some broader understanding. Was there some broader understanding pulling at the edges of his mind, seeking a shape from scraps like sperm numbers?

His mind returned to the strange feeling he experienced last night and this morning. "Chest discomfort," he thought.

"One of the vague universal symptoms of heart attacks." Could it be that? "I'll have it checked out first thing next week, or maybe just after the State Biology meeting week after next," he promised himself.

He glanced up and noticed a red-tailed hawk sailing up over the trees on the left side of the roadway. Likely it was the same one that had the nest in the trees off to the right of the road. She would certainly be protecting this territory, and was probably searching for food for herself or the nestlings in the trees. From high above she was angling downward toward the broad left shoulder of the bypass, coming almost straight toward the Jeep, but still far away.

Out of the corner of his eye he was momentarily aware of a rusty pickup parked on the rough grass, but it was the hawk that got his attention. As it reached the spot where the shoulder of the road played out, and the bank dropped sharply down to the creek, she flinched. That momentary awkward flap of wings was the last thing Clarence saw, and a burning pain in his shoulder and neck was his last feeling as he crossed over Grovetown Road.

* * *

He could hear quiet voices, almost secretive, drifting in from unknown distances, out of a dreamy haze. One sounded like Susan, but where was she? Where was *he*? He stirred, and pain shot through his right leg when he tried to move, through his eyes when he tried to open them. His left shoulder and neck felt bulky, stiff as if wrapped in something.

He called, "Susan?" but his voice sounded strange.

He heard an answer, a voice that sounded distant, different. "Clarence, I'm here, honey. How do you feel?"

"Where are we? What happened?"

"There was an accident," she said in a quiet, measured voice, "You were on the way to the dentist's office."

"I've got to go, it's nearly time for class," he said weakly, but with some determination.

"No, Clarence, it's eight o'clock Friday night. You had class this afternoon," she said.

"Where are we," he repeated. He could see, but the things he saw made no sense, gave no clue. Susan, in a vaguely familiar beige skirt and matching blouse, stood in front of a strange chair. A television, no sound, hanging from the ceiling, showed a car chase that could have been from the news or a cop-detective movie.

"The hospital," Susan said. "You had an accident. Ran off the road on the north bypass."

Clarence stayed quiet for several minutes, trying to clear his head, understand where he was, how he got here. "Was it a heart attack?" The wrapping on his chest and shoulder, the pain in his leg. He vaguely recalled that arteries are taken from patients' legs to repair heart arteries. He also had a hazy memory of concern about chest discomfort.

Susan murmured some reassurance, but he couldn't grasp her words as he sank again into the mist from which he emerged.

When Clarence awoke again his mouth was dry as cotton. He hurt in several places that weren't completely separate. And he was hungry!

Except for the quiet drone of air conditioning, traffic or some combination of machinery, there was no sound. Nobody around. "I'm in a hospital room" he decided , "but how did I get here?" He started to get up, but winced at the pull of the intravenous tube and needle. The pain throughout his body multiplied ten-fold. He lay back, closed his eyes, tried to think.

As soon as he closed his eyes he heard his name, "Professor Harris," in an unfamiliar voice. Startled, he opened his eyes to see a man in a white smock over a white shirt and maroon tie. Just behind him was a large man of about forty in a business suit with a serious, tight grimace on his face. The tight-lipped grimace almost broke into a smile of greeting when Clarence's eyes fell on it, but it quickly returned to a serious, "I'll-wait-my-turn" look.

The man in the white smock called again more quietly and slowly than before, "Professor Harris, how are you feeling?"

"Where's Susan?" he asked. The last person he wanted to talk to, without any mooring, as if he had just come into the world, was a stranger in a white coat backed up by a tight-lipped businessman.

"She's just down the hall at the coffee shop, probably on her way back here. I'm Dr. Steele, an intern here at Clayton Medical Center. This is Detective James. He would like to ask you a few questions."

Clarence knew he wasn't going to talk, not before Susan returned to help, to give some support. He felt baffled. What business could a detective have here? What had happened that he knew nothing about?

"Mr. Steele... er... Dr. Steele, I don't know anything, why I'm here, how I got here." Talk was labor, a struggle. "Last thing I remember I was standing in front of my class at the college. Could I have something to drink, my mouth is dry? I'm starving."

Clarence glanced behind Mr. James and saw a familiar figure come through the door. "Susan, can you tell me what's going on?" He struggled to make his voice loud enough to be heard. "Why are these people here? Why am I here?"

Susan came over to the bed, took his hand, smoothed his hair, and said, "Clarence, honey, you look much better this morning. This is Dr. Steele with the hospital, and Mr. James from the Clayton police department. You had an accident on the bypass yesterday, and Mr. James is checking on it."

Clarence watched Dr. Steele take advantage of this conversation to pick up the clipboard from the foot of the bed and check the medicines and schedule.

Clarence tried to reach out to Susan. "How long have I been here? I don't remember anything since class. I don't see how I can answer any questions. I need something to drink and eat."

"They brought you in about three o'clock yesterday afternoon," Susan explained. "Well, you would be hungry. I'll go get you some breakfast."

"What time is it?" Clarence asked as she turned to go.

"Almost eleven in the morning."

"What day?"

"Saturday. Be back in a minute. You just stay where you are!" And she laughed, but it sounded rather a forced laugh.

Dr. Steele leaned forward. "Professor Harris, your injuries are not too serious, but we will need to keep you here another day or two. You're lucky to have no fractures from the accident, just some serious bruises, a slight concussion, and a bullet wound beneath the left collarbone. It was about as clean as a bullet wound can be. Passed almost all the way through without hitting any bones or vital organs. It'll be plenty sore, but should heal without much problem."

"Bullet... what!!!" Clarence's mind stopped at "bullet". He didn't hear another word the doctor said. "Wait, doctor, did you say I've been shot? I thought it was a heart attack, and I crashed the Jeep! Last thing I remember I was standing in front of my class, talking. Wait until my wife gets back. She'll know what's going on." Clarence's mind was in chaos. Heart trouble, auto accident, bullet wound – and he remembered none of it. He tried to raise his head and shoulders, and the pain seared through his body. He winced, moaned aloud and fell back down.

"You need to settle down and get some rest," the doctor told him. "Your heart's fine. You're going to be as good as new in a few weeks."

Susan returned and said, "Clarence, food is on the way, but

they'll only let you have liquids for now. They'll bring coffee and juice and maybe some Jello."

He was hardly listening. "Susan, what's this about a bullet in me? What's happened?"

"They don't know much about it, yet," Susan told him softly, "but your Jeep ran off the north bypass. That's why detective James is here. He's been trying to find out what happened, and needs to ask you some questions. Do you think you'll feel up to it after some coffee and juice?"

He certainly didn't feel up to questions. He had no memory after the middle of his class lecture. Now he had no hunger for food, not after hearing about being shot, but his mouth felt dry as ever.

Lieutenant James, the large, serious-looking man in the business suit, spoke for the first time since coming into the room. "Mister... uh... Professor... Harris, I just need to ask a couple of questions to help me get started on this. We can talk more later, when you're feeling better. All I need to know now is if you saw anything unusual on the bypass at Grovetown Road yesterday."

"I don't even remember being at Grovetown Road, or on the bypass," he said.

"Do you know of anyone who might have it in for you, who might try to hurt you?"

"Detective, I don't know of anyone who would cuss me under their breath, much less try to kill me."

"Have you had any disagreements with any of the people

you work with, or neighbors or relatives?"

"I don't remember any." Clarence glanced at Susan, a questioning look. Detective James followed the glance and Susan shook her head.

Just then a large lady in white came in with a tray of coffee and juice, and sat it on the swing-around shelf attached to the stand by the bed. Susan began opening the juice and sweetening the coffee.

Lieutenant James shook his head. "Okay, I can't see we're going to get anywhere right now. I'll leave it a couple of days, I guess. You sure you don't remember anything from yesterday, Professor?"

Clarence shook his head slowly and painfully. "Nothing. Was that when it happened?"

Susan spoke up. "You taught class at your regular time yesterday, and then left for Dr. Simpson's office for a checkup. I called you while you were in class and left a reminder. Did you listen to my call on your answering machine?"

"I don't remember leaving class."

Detective James came close. "Just one more question, Professor. "You ran off the shoulder of the bypass at Grovetown Road. Was there anything unusual at the intersection, anybody try to contact you, run you off the road, blow a horn, anything?"

"I don't think so. I have this vague memory of seeing an old pickup and...yes...a hawk flying toward me."

"A hawk?" Detective James sounded perplexed.

"My husband studies hawks as part of his work at Clawson

University," Susan explained.

"I see," the detective said, probably not understanding at all. "What about this pickup?"

Clarence tried to recall exactly what he'd seen. But it was like trying to remember a dream. The memory deserted him as he attempted to hold onto it.

"Can you recall the color?" the detective asked.

Clarence shook his head. "I'm not even sure I saw anything," he said quietly. "Look, Detective, I'm tired. I'll write it down if anything comes back to me. Okay?"

Lieutenant James nodded, somewhat reluctantly. "You be sure you do," he said. "I'll see you later. Thank you for your time and trouble, Professor."

After the detective left, Clarence felt relieved to be alone with Susan, but all the talk and excitement was making him weak, confused, resigned to sleep. Maybe things would be better when he woke up. Maybe this was a dream that he could laugh at later. He sipped his orange juice through a straw and drank half cup of coffee. It was really what he needed to refresh his parched throat.

An old pickup? A hawk? Memories like dry sand running away through his fingers. All he wanted now was sleep.

The Lottery

He was in a large warehouse, in the middle of an open 18-wheeler trailer filled with tickets. Up to his shoulders in some kind of tickets. Millions and millions of tickets, nothing but tickets. He didn't have a clue where he was or why.

"What is this" he asked the man standing on the dock next to where the truck was parked. The portly man, dressed in light blue coveralls with vertical white pinstripes, gave the appearance of an old-time railroad man. He even had a railroad cap. Clarence could make out a circular red emblem on the breast of the coveralls, but not the words surrounding it. The man possessed the confidence of a salesman who has all the answers and the polish of long experience.

"Lottery tickets," the man said. "Three hundred million dreams, all in one pile. You ever see such a thing? You won't ever see it again, not this many tickets in one place."

"Lotteries aren't handled this way," Clarence thought. To be honest, he didn't have a clue how the lottery was managed.

"You're the man. You're going to make somebody's dream come true."

"Yeah, right," Clarence, decided, "if they're dreaming of a load of recycled paper."

He picked up some of the tickets and let them flutter to the top of the pile. "Why am I here," he asked. "I need to be home. I have a thousand things to do."

"We only need you for a few minutes. Believe me, you're going to make some ticket holder unbelievably happy." The man in charge stood erect, his stomach sticking out considerably farther than his chest. His stance reminded Clarence of the old-time comedian, W.C. Fields. "You've been selected to draw the winning ticket in the Grand Regional that will pay the winner eighty-seven million dollars."

"You're kidding," Clarence said. "Lotteries aren't decided like this. There has to be a computer program or something that draws the numbers. The drawing has to be random. Every ticket buyer must have an equal chance."

"Oh, they do. Every ticket in this truck has been through a random shake. See that randomizer machine over there?"

Clarence looked in the direction the man turned, and saw what looked like a concrete mixer, but several times as large. It took up a big section in the huge warehouse they were in.

"They went through that shaker a few minutes ago, and are now thoroughly mixed," the man continued. "So no matter which ticket you come up with, it'll be a random pick. You can pick one in front of you, behind you, it doesn't matter. The tickets are identified only by numbers. Never bet on the lottery in your life, have you?"

Clarence shook his head.

"Wouldn't matter," the man said, "but we picked you to insure against bias. We guessed you wouldn't even know what a lottery ticket looked like."

Clarence thought quickly. He was going to make somebody incredibly rich, just by picking up a ticket.

Why him? They could have a machine select the number. The whole idea was trivial. Such vast riches based on a random selection of a single ticket. "What happens next to all these tickets," he asked.

"Well, the moment you select the winner all the rest are worthless, 'relegated to the scrap heap of history,' as the saying goes."

Clarence doubted that anyone had ever said anything close, and certainly not about scraps of paper. "It doesn't seem right that all of these tickets are worth the same just now, and because I hand one to you, all but that one are worthless. It's like magic — the feeble wealth of millions becomes the fantastic wealth of one, and the pitiful value of the millions disappears."

"It's called gambling," said the lottery master. "It's a fortune waiting for someone to collect."

Clarence plunged his hand deep into the mass of paper.

Recovery and Investigation

Clarence opened his eyes with feelings of confusion and relief. There was no sign of lottery tickets. Must have been a dream. He quickly sensed a hubbub around him — talking, laughing — but in a quiet kind of respect for a hospital room. Oh yes, he was in a hospital room. He remembered that he'd been told he was in an accident... no, that he'd been shot... definitely shot. He could feel the pain and constriction in his shoulder and chest.

"Dad, how are you feeling?" It was his son Ed. That's the first question everybody asks, Clarence thought. They know I feel ready to die, but they ask anyway. I guess it's because they don't know what to say. *And* they don't realize I just woke up from a senseless dream.

Ed grinned. "You and the Jeep had it out on the bypass, I hear. It was about time to trade that old rattle trap, anyway." This was his way to be casual in all circumstances, a burst of nonchalant bluster to cover any situation. It suited Clarence fine. Better than pity or talking details of his problems.

Clarence's daughter, Erin, pushed Ed aside. Clarence felt

her hand on his head and saw the excruciating concern in her face. He thought immediately about the twin girls, Christine and Catherine and wondered where they were. Probably with their dad. He smiled to himself. Maybe there wasn't too much wrong with his memory after all.

"Daddy, I'm so sorry. Tom and I came as soon as we heard," Erin sobbed, squatting, with her face in the bed sheet next to his good shoulder. The tears came and stopped the flow of words. From Erin, the tears always came.

He laid his right arm across her shoulder. "I'm okay," he said, "You didn't have to drive all this way. You could have just called." He knew better, but he wanted to minimize his own problems. He knew, too, what was coming next.

"But, Dad, you could have been killed!" It sounded like a complaint and an accusation. Female anguish.

"Well, I dodged a...." He couldn't take it back, he didn't mean to say it, and didn't know how to finish it.

The awkward expressions for his well-being weren't helping him or the children, but he was glad to see them here. Whatever the circumstances, he would rather have them around than away. It wasn't pleasant now, though, because he had too many things to sort out, part of which was the terrible pain.

The love and concern that was thick in the room would be welcome and enjoyable in other circumstances. Right now he needed time alone to think, and time with Susan to get her help in recovering from all that had happened.

He watched Susan come over, helping to calm Erin. Perhaps she sensed the need to clear the room of as much emotion as possible. "Erin and Tom came late yesterday, and Ed got here this morning," she explained. "They'll be staying at the house for a day or two."

"I went to see the Jeep this morning," said Ed. "It was torn up pretty bad. Lucky you weren't hurt worse."

Erin started sobbing again.

"Ed, why don't you go down to the nurses' station and see if they can bring your dad something to eat or drink," Susan said with a dismissive tone. "Clarence, are you hungry? They said you could have soft scrambled eggs, oatmeal, something like that."

"Scrambled eggs and grits would be fine, but I would really like some coffee."

Ed ambled off down the hall.

Clarence turned to Erin. "Where's Tom?"

"He's with the kids at the house," Susan said. "He'll come down this afternoon."

Clarence liked Erin's husband Tom a lot, not just for the way he fit in with the Harris's, but because he was such a level-headed fellow, easy to talk to, industrious, and devoted to Erin and the children. After eating a light breakfast and chatting with the three people he was closest to, he told Susan he felt sleepy.

Susan turned to the others. "We're going home now and eat some lunch. We'll be back this afternoon." Turning to Clarence, she said, "Detective James called and asked if you could talk this afternoon. Do you feel up to it?"

"I don't want to talk," Clarence said.

"If you can, you ought to," Susan told him. "They need to find out what happened as soon as they can."

"How long before he comes?"

"He said three o'clock. It's eleven now, so you need some time to rest."

"I've got more rest than I want already. But, okay, maybe I can get some sleep before then."

* * *

Clarence woke up at a quarter to one. He knew, because an orderly was banging around, and he asked him the time. Within five minutes a nurse appeared, to take his temperature and check his bandages. "Mister Harris, we need to give you a bath pretty soon. You feel up to that?"

Clarence smiled. "That would help me a lot. That detective is supposed to come at three. Could you do it before then?"

"I'll be back in about five minutes," she promised.

When the nurse and a helper returned, the agony of the bath gave Clarence second thoughts. The moving and turning required for the bath caused more pain than he had felt in a long time, and it told him he was in no condition to be up and around soon.

The nurse obviously noticed this and said, "We'll be back in the morning to get you up, and see if you can move about a little. Can't let you shrivel up in bed."

As soon as the nurse left, Clarence felt better than he had since he landed here Friday afternoon. His bed had been raised at the head so that he was sitting up, kind of. He was ready for the detective physically, but he didn't have any idea what to say to whatever kind of questions Lieutenant James might have.

A light knock on the door announced the detective as his frame appeared around the jamb. He was built like a lineman on a football team, medium height and stocky, but about forty pounds heavier than playing weight. He wore a light gray business suit with a plain blue tie.

"Professor Harris, you look much better today. Hope you're feeling as good as you look."

"Detective, I feel good, except about whatever it is you're going to ask me. I'm afraid I'm not even sure now about seeing a pickup. All I can remember is the hawk."

"Don't worry about it," Detective James said. "Whatever you can tell me will help, but we have other leads we're following. Last time I talked to you, you were still pretty much under with shock and anesthetics. Forget that old pickup for the moment. Let's think about the hawk. That might help your recall other things. You told me you saw a hawk flying overhead. Can you still remember it?"

Clarence nodded. "She was flying toward me. She seemed to dart at the last...last thing I remember."

The detective laughed. "I forgot you're an expert on birds. Not many people would know a male red-tailed from a female. Tell me, where was the hawk? Over the bypass, off to the side, where? Was it close or far away?"

"She was over the left shoulder of the bypass, and had just cleared the trees where they play out at the intersection."

"And is that where he reacted, darted, flapped, or whatever?" James asked.

"Yes, she not he."

"Oh yeah, do you think that the hawk was reacting to something or someone on the side of the highway?"

Clarence suddenly felt that the detective knew something more. "Could be," he said. "Do you know what she might have reacted to?"

"We have some indication that someone was recently on the shoulder of the bypass, where it drops down to the creek."

"So you think there really was a rusty old pickup, and someone might have shot at me from there?"

"It's possible. It could be that the hawk was reacting to the shot. Whoever did the shooting could have been anywhere, but I'm investigating the pickup. Have you remembered anything else about it? Color perhaps?"

"I told you, I'm not even sure I saw a pickup. I know I had a memory once, but it kind of slid away. All I can see clearly is the hawk."

The detective laughed. "Shame you're not more interested in vehicles than birds. Did you talk to anyone after class, or on the way to the dentist? I mean, after you left the campus"?

"Let's see." Clarence frowned. "I remember stopping at a station for gas just before I got on the bypass."

"Where?" James asked quickly.

"It was that little cheap-gas convenience store on Sawyer Street. 'Pump Jump', or something like that. Run by an Indian-looking guy."

"I know the place. He is an Indian, Asian Indian. Did you talk to him?"

"Just said hello. I was in a hurry."

"What time was it?" James asked.

"Well my class ends at 2:05, so it must have been about 2:20 or 2:30. I don't remember stopping for anything else. Just went by my office and dropped off some books and papers, and checked my answering machine."

"Were there any messages, any unusual ones, anybody you didn't know?"

"One message. My wife reminding me about the dentist appointment."

"Was there anyone at the convenience store while you were there?"

"Just some homeless guy buying lottery tickets ahead of me."

"Did he say anything to you? Did you talk?"

Clarence had to think. "No," he said at last, "I was in a hurry to get to the dentist, and he took forever to pay."

"Did he have an old pickup?"

"I shouldn't think so. Not to look at him. I assumed he was walking. Come to think of it, I was the only one at the pumps."

"Were you upset at him?"

"What's that got to do with anything?" Clarence felt irritated for the first time. Investigators like James had to cover all the bases, but it seemed useless to talk about a conversation with a homeless man that never took place anyway.

"Probably nothing, Professor, but unless the person who took a shot was using you for target practice, or satisfying some random urge, we need to find a motive."

"You can rule out the guy buying the ticket. He couldn't have got to the bypass in time!" Clarence snapped.

Detective James looked unruffled "He might if he had an old pickup round the corner. I'm not trying to tie you to anybody, or them to you. At this stage I have to look at everything. Is there anything else you can remember about the afternoon?"

"Nothing. Let me ask you something, Detective James." Clarence didn't really want do this, but he'd blurted it out and was too far along to quit. He knew that one of his self-confessed faults was starting a line of talk, before thinking about where it would lead. "Do you play the lottery?"

The detective's eyes widened and his hands shifted his notepad a little higher, as if ready to write something new. His tight-lipped, straight-across mouth actually bowed upwards into a frown-grimace. "Yeah, a little. Actually I buy four a week. Two for Mattie and two for me. Why do you ask?"

"I'm not sure," Clarence said slowly. "That homeless fellow I saw Friday — it was Friday wasn't it? — was buying lottery tickets. Since I've been in here I've had the craziest dream about the lottery. I know nothing about the lottery. I don't even know why I brought it up."

The large detective came closer. "Let me tell you, stress and injury, hospitals and jails bring out all kinds of crazy jangles and irrelevant thoughts and behavior. Believe me, I've seen it all. Just last week I saw this fellow strung out on drugs; thought he was a tree. Stood straight in the corner with his arms out and his branches — his hands — hanging down. Whatever they gave you for pain and that shoulder of yours can make you see hell, heaven, or your Mama, while you're fighting in the dark. Don't give it a second thought, Professor."

Clarence said nothing. He'd talked enough.

The detective snapped his notebook shut. "I have to go now, but I need to tell you that until we find out who did the shooting, we want you to be very careful. I've asked the doctor to keep you in the hospital a couple more days, for your safety."

Clarence wanted to protest, but decided against it. "I need to wait until Susan gets back," he said to himself. "She's thinking a lot clearer than I am just now. As always."

After Detective James had gone, Clarence tried to put together what had happened in the last three days. He remembered now the class on Friday and then later, up until getting on the bypass. He tried to recall the problems he was mulling on the way to the dentist's office, but they wouldn't come to him.

He did recall one item that was on his mind before class. Susan's car was in the shop. She'd been left stranded and must have been at a loss when she got the call about his being taken to the hospital. A pang of concern for her stuck in his mind for several seconds, but he knew she wouldn't have been bothered by the problem for long before she arranged for someone to take her to the hospital. It was probably Blanche Benoit from next door.

He could hear voices in the hall. Susan, Erin and Tom came in looking relaxed and well fed. "Well, you seem better already," Susan said with a smile. "What did they do to you? You look cleaner somehow, rested,"

He really did feel better, in spite of the questions from Detective James. "I had a bath. This beautiful young nurse cleaned me and changed my bandages. She was so gentle, it didn't hurt at all." He said it with mock seriousness.

"Yeah, you wouldn't have noticed if she twisted that arm behind your back," Susan said, just as mockish. "I saw her in the hall this morning. She's just the type to kill your pain."

Clarence certainly couldn't tell Susan now that the nurse that bathed him was fifty-five and weighed 220 pounds. He just grinned. "How are the kids? Who's keeping them? Oh, must be Ed. I hope they haven't climbed that pecan tree in the back."

"Oh, Daddy," said Erin, "they'll be okay. How are you feeling? Have you had lunch?"

"I can't remember," he said truthfully. "I'd sure like something to drink."

"I'll get you something, Mister Harris," said Tom, speaking for the first time, "how about a Coke?" He turned and went out into the hall.

"Susan, your car's in the shop. We need to go get it," Clarence said.

"Well, Albert, we already did." Susan wagged a finger at him. "Tom went with me to get it yesterday. Nothing to worry about." She smiled and he knew she was giving him the berries about his illogical offer to help get the car in his condition. She usually called him "Albert" as in Einstein when he made stupid remarks. She called him that often enough that there was no question what she meant, and often enough that the rest of the family knew the full meaning. He never took offense. Now it was a sign that she and the others were feeling better about him, and not quite so worried.

Well, time to change that, Clarence thought. "Detective James was here a little while ago," he said. "He thinks the rusty pickup could be important, and he wants us to be careful."

"But, Daddy, what can we do?" said Erin, obviously shaken. "We can't just stay inside the house all the time."

"I think the best thing for you, Tom, and the kids, is to go home. The danger, if any, is not likely for you."

"But what about you and Mom?"

"I don't think the danger is very real," Susan said, "and I don't believe the police think so either. Otherwise they would have warned us before now. I suspect the person who shot at your father is some sort of kook who doesn't even know him." She turned to Clarence. "How could someone have known you'd have been driving by at that time, or even on that route?

By the way, who knew you were going to the dentist?"

"I didn't tell anybody, not even the secretary," Clarence said. "You know it's strange that Detective James didn't ask me that." He thought for a moment about the homeless man buying the ticket at the convenience store, and wondered if he *was* somehow involved, or if the clerk could have called the shooter. It was so preposterous that he dismissed it quickly. He certainly wasn't going to voice such thoughts in this company.

Tom came back with a large Coke, and Clarence downed half of it quickly. "Thanks, Tom."

Tom nodded. "Anything else I can do for you, Mister Harris?"

"Teach my class tomorrow," Clarence said, grinning. "Other than that, I don't believe there is anything. Oh yeah, take your wife and kids back to Jefferson City, home."

Tom looked startled. Erin smiled. "Daddy says the police think there may be danger from whoever shot him."

Clarence looked at Tom. "Probably not, but just the same, I think it would be better if you two were home. You can't do anything for me here. Sergeant Harris here can stand watch." He looked at "Sergeant Harris". Her fake, broad smile flashed quickly before she turned to Erin and Tom for some goodbye chatter.

After they left, Clarence had plenty of questions for Susan. "Did our pastor come by since I've been here?"

Susan nodded. "While you were asleep yesterday. He prayed for you at your beside. He said he'll call again, when you're awake."

"I'd like that. It's good to know someone is praying for me – as well as you." This might be a scary time, but he had long known the value of prayer. "Who operated on me to take the bullet out?"

"Dr. Marchant. Remember, he took your appendix out five years ago? He happened to be on duty when you came in on Friday."

"Has anyone called from the University? I need to see about my class and the meetings I'm supposed to attend next week."

"I called George Stoddard earlier today. He said he'll call you later."

Clarence should have known. Susan had thought of everything, arranged everything. "What do I have to worry about?" he said to himself.

* * *

Monday morning raised Clarence's spirits, although the wound in his shoulder and chest began to hurt more. His medication had been reduced and he was feeling that deep, throbbing pain in the muscles and tissues the bullet had torn through. His mind seemed clearer now, and he knew that before long he would be up and back into the routine he loved so much, the people and duties he was comfortable with. He'd been able to arrange with George Stoddard, his Department Chairman, late yesterday for someone to teach his biology class, and to notify the state Biology Conference organizers that he wouldn't be able to attend and present his lecture.

So with two large loads off his mind he turned to his most pressing problems: sorting out this hospital confinement and finding out about what had happened to him. He needed Susan's help.

He didn't have to wait long. She came in at quarter-to-nine, and what she had with her helped his spirits more. In a small shallow basket were two fried egg sandwiches on toasted bread, just as he liked them. Susan had warned him by phone not to eat the hospital breakfast, so he guessed something good was coming.

The excellent food and the presence of Susan raised his spirits even more. She sat on the edge of the bed, took his hand, and kissed him lightly on the lips. "I know everything is going to be okay, soon," she whispered. "And our pastor and all the folks at church are praying for you."

He felt emotion welling up within. "Susan, I don't know what I'd do without you. Every time I get in trouble, you're there to bail me out or hold things steady until the storm blows over. As long as you're around, everything will be okay, soon."

"You have to stop worrying, Clarence. There's a kook out there somewhere who doesn't know who he shot, and he's not bothered. It may as well have been a rabbit for all he cares. You had the bad luck to come along at just the wrong time. Think about what you're going to do when you get out of here. Worry about that hawk nesting on the bypass, not what happened to you out there. Think about those twin girls who were asking for

Grandpa over the weekend, when they saw everybody but you."

"You're probably right. But I sure hope that Sherlock James comes up with an answer soon."

The large nurse who gave him a bath yesterday came in. "Feeling better this morning, Mister Harris? Remember, I promised some exercise this morning. Do you feel up to it?"

"No, but let's do it anyway."

The nurse smiled brightly. "Carlos will be here in a few minutes to help us. Is there anything I can get for you in the meantime?"

"A little more coffee. What kind of exercise am I in for?" Clarence asked.

"We're just going to get you up and walk around a little. Then we'll maybe see if you can bath yourself. Think you can?"

Clarence didn't answer. He glanced at Susan who was enjoying a head-down diverted smile about Clarence's bath by this "beautiful nurse" who could probably bath a buffalo.

A few minutes later the exercise session filled him with excruciating pain, not just in his shoulder, but in his right knee which was bluish-black, and his right rib-cage which had a tender discolored spot the size of a softball. He was surprised how many bruises and small cuts he had. Although he had his seatbelt on, the welts across his chest and stomach showed that, he had bounced around as the Jeep rolled over once, or maybe even twice.

After walking halfway down the hall with Carlos and the nurse holding on to him, he was weak and exhausted when he got back into the bed, which somehow had gotten clean sheets while he was gone. The bath would have to wait until afternoon.

With the nurse gone and Susan off to do some errands, Clarence was alone with the jumbled ends of his daily routines. He started to sort them as best he could. He set a goal of Friday to get home and start back in his daily life. By then they surely would have found what was behind his "accident". And he should be ready to reclaim his class. Could he drive by then, or would Susan have to taxi him everywhere? How could he visit his research sites that required considerable climbing, ducking and weaving among branches and briars? It was a critical time to collect data on the nesting and parenting habits of the hawks he was intent on learning more about.

This hawk-watching dilemma brought back memories of the disdain his father Ruston had expressed before he passed away. His father had never been able to accept his son's research. Studying the habits of hawks, and especially talking fondly about birds that were the enemies of farm chickens in earlier times, confounded his father and weakened a bond that was otherwise strong and mutually treasured. Several times his father jokingly, but with hidden seriousness, told Clarence he should get a real job.

He wandered off into the back roads of his memory, in spite of the need to concentrate on his recovery. He wondered if Aunt Anne, his "new" mother, was aware of his predicament. He made a mental note to ask Susan to call, or to get Aunt Anne's number for him.

He was just getting back to business when lunch came. Along with it came Detective James. Clarence felt hungry and didn't let the presence of the detective keep him from uncovering the tray, arranging the utensils and tasting his drink.

"Professor Harris, I think I have some good news."

Clarence brightened. "I could use some."

"We found tire marks leading up to that road shoulder where we think the shooter was. A resident said she saw an old pickup go up that road last Friday. See, you were right. But at least she had a good memory."

Clarence felt this comment was directed at him. He was about to protest, but let it pass.

"She gave us a good description. Well, we found it and questioned the owner."

"Who is he?"

"An old man who lives out on this back-country road over near the Lyons County line. We've arrested him and have him in the jail downtown."

"What did he say?"

"Nothing that makes any sense, but his tires match the tracks we found."

"But there could have been others up that road besides him, couldn't there?"

Detective James nodded. "But according to the couple of families that live on that road, hardly anyone goes on past the houses up near the bypass. That's one reason the woman was so clear about the description; almost nobody goes past her house."

Clarence supposed it was good news. "If it was him, why do you think he did it?"

"He's probably crazy. Maybe he doesn't know why he did it. May not even *know* he did it."

"So how can you be sure it was him?"

James sounded a little too confident. "There are a couple more things we need to check. We're going to examine his rifle to see if it's been fired lately. We can check his shoe prints against the ones we found at the scene. We can even check the bullet against his rifle, although the doc said there was only a fragment of it that hit you. It broke in the impact with the windshield."

"I have an idea," said Clarence.

The detective looked surprised.

"You say he's wacky, right?"

James nodded.

"And he claims not to remember?"

"That's right." Detective James sounded interested.

"Why not take him out to the spot where you think he was when I was shot, and get his reaction?"

The detective's eyes lit up. "Professor, you may have something there. We'll give it a try."

"When you get him out there," Clarence said, "ask him about the shooting in an off-hand way. Maybe you can catch him off guard – if he has enough brain to be on guard."

Detective James got up to leave. "You ought to give this

detective work a try, Professor. I think you'd be good at it."

"I couldn't stand badgering broken-up people in hospital beds," Clarence said with a smile.

James left the room with a chuckle, the first Clarence had heard from him. He rolled slightly to his left and reached across his body with his right hand for the phone to call Susan, but jolted with a pain that made him grunt aloud. The news would have to wait.

Discovery

Friday morning Dr. Marchant gave Clarence and Susan the good news. He'd made excellent progress and could go home that afternoon. Clarence was too realistic to think he could get back into his routine immediately, but at least he'd become ambulatory: walking still with some pain, but walking. He had to sit up most of the time, catching up on his school work, calling people he worked with, planning to get back in the woods to continue his work with hawks. But after being away from class for a week, the priority was to get ready to be back there on Monday.

When they got home Susan ordered him to bed. He knew she was right, and he felt tired. But he couldn't sleep. He began reflecting on the coming week, wondering if his class was on schedule and what he'd do first when he went back. He remembered the end of the class before his fateful trip to the dentist. The question Bill Carter, no Ben Carter, asked. "How many sperm does a man produce in an average sex act?" He remembered his reaction, his feeling that some question arose in his own mind, infinitely more important than the number of sperm.

Suddenly he knew what had been playing at the edges of his mind. What is the chance that a given person would be born? *Me* for instance? The union of the one female egg and one male sperm produces a baby, a person, right? But the chance for that potential person is small if there is a large number of sperm. The more sperm produced, the less the chance there is of that one sperm fertilizing the egg; so the less the chance of that person, me, being born.

"What was the chance I had at the moment of conception?" he wondered aloud. "That's the importance of Ben Carter's question. How many sperm are competing for that one egg? Where can I find the answer?"

He had no doubt that the answer was available, but where? He remembered that several years ago he and Susan had bought a medical handbook, published by a famous hospital. He struggled to remember. The Mayo Clinic! The answer might be in there. If not, surely it would be easy to find in the college library.

Clarence got up, struggled slowly down the stairs, and went to the bookcase in the den where he found the *Mayo Clinic Family Health Book*. He sat down slowly and carefully in the large easy chair with the tall lamp beside it. He turned on the lamp and opened the book to the index. Handling the large book was a challenge, because his left arm was still so painful as to be almost useless. He looked for *Sperm*, found the page number and then paged slowly with his right thumb and forefinger until he found the section entitled *Reproduction*, subsection *Spermatogenesis*. He scanned the descriptions of sperm and their formation. And there, at the end of the section, was the number he was looking for. *The number of sperm produced per ejaculation averages one-half billion.*

"Damn," he said softly but emphatically, stunned. He leaned back in the chair staring at the book, not seeing anything, his injuries temporarily forgotten.

"My chance of being born was one in five hundred million. If another sperm had fertilized my mother's egg, another child would have been born. My chance would have been gone. Zero. And there were five hundred million of those sperm. I was the one, one in five hundred million. The lottery of lotteries!"

A line from his troubled dream in the hospital came back: *"The moment you select the winner all the rest are worthless, 'relegated to the scrap heap of history,' as the saying goes."*

"All those sperm wasted except the fateful one. What a blessing, what a gift, what a miracle!"

He closed the book, put it aside, and headed back to bed. Halfway down the hallway he looked up to see Susan.

"What are you doing, pacing the house?" she demanded. "You need to be upstairs in the bed. You look like you just took a call from a ghost."

"Actually, I just got a wake-up call. It might have been from a ghost. Come back to the bedroom and I'll tell you."

She took his best arm, the right one, and helped him up the stairs.

"I've just made an amazing discovery," he told her. "It floored me. I don't know what to make of it."

After he was settled in bed, with Susan seated on the edge holding his hand, he started. "I've just found out how incredibly lucky I am to be alive."

"Clarence, you've got to get that off your mind. It's over now. You'll be as good as new in a week or two." Turning mock cheerful, she said, "You could look at it the other way. You've been unlucky. If you'd been a few minutes earlier or later, you would never have been hit."

"No, no, no," he protested, "I've just realized that I was conceived and born against unbelievable odds."

Susan started to interrupt, but he kept on, "So were you. Do you want to know how unbelievable?"

"Clarence, I really don't know what you're talking about. Are you still troubled about the confusion over your mother and Aunt Anne? Over your adoption? I thought you accepted the fact that Aunt Anne is your real mother. You seemed pleased about it. It's not that, is it? What's bothering you?"

"You understand enough biology to know that when a baby is conceived, it results from a sperm from the father fertilizing the egg from the mother."

"Clarence, even small kids know that. But go on."

"You probably don't know — I certainly didn't — that there are five hundred million sperm competing for that one egg. You and I were born against odds of five hundred million to one. I don't know how that makes you feel, but it's knocked me over.

For you and me, actually for every living soul, it's an absolute miracle."

He waited to see her reaction. It was mild, non-committal. "Okay, I see the point, but don't people know that already? Why would it surprise anyone in biology, even you, and especially doctors?"

"Well, it's surprised me beyond anything in a long time, maybe ever. You and I are religious people, Susan. Have you ever heard about the blessing of being born?"

"Well, I've heard of the miracle of birth. In some churches we christen babies, celebrate their birth, dedicate their lives to God."

"Yeah, but that's the miracle of the appearance of the baby in the world. It's a miracle for the *parents*. The miracle for the *baby* is that it overcame odds of five hundred million to one. I'll bet you not one in five hundred million babies grow up to know the real miracle in that birth. Besides that, christening is a dedication of the new life to Christ. So it's more a ceremony of dedication than one of gratitude. Even if it were a celebration of birth, it would be for gratitude of the parents. For them the reason for gratitude is important, but to the baby it's everything, existence, the difference between the greatest gift and nothing."

It seemed a long time before Susan spoke again. At last she said, "Clarence, I don't think I can ever remember you being so eloquent or so serious." She took his head in her lap and put her finger to his lips. "Let's talk about this later. Something big is happening in your life. Some revelation. And I'm here for you."

Clarence felt a great swell of warmth and love surge thorough his body as he drifted off into a peaceful sleep.

* * *

Saturday morning dawned bright and clear, lifting his spirits. From the kitchen he heard familiar sounds of breakfast preparation as he struggled to get up. The pain in his shoulder was still intense, but getting slightly less each day. His knee injury was much better, most of the swelling gone, but still stiff, discolored and painful. He limped slowly to the kitchen.

"Good morning," he called in a low voice, trying to sound as normal as possible.

Susan turned, looking surprised. She walked quickly to him, encircled him with her arms, and kissed him firmly. The pain in his ribs and shoulder made him wince.

Susan drew back. "I'm so sorry!"

He held her with his right arm and put his face against her neck and shoulder. He held her there. "I love you more than ever. I hope I wasn't too strange last night."

She tightened her arms slightly around him. "I know you, Clarence Harris, you've always been strange. And I love strange." Straightening, she said, "How about an omelet?"

"Just what I need." Now he knew everything was okay, the old routine back.

"You want Jamaican Hellfire or Texas Pete?" she asked over her shoulder from the stove.

"A little Texas Pete. I'll probably be sorry later"

"You never complained about it before. Oh, you mean because of the injury?"

"Especially because of that, but sometimes I have heartburn. Nothing too serious. And at least I know it's not my heart."

"Here, I'll let you control the fire," she said, putting the bottle of hot sauce down in front of him.

In five minutes he was enjoying the wonderful omelet with a little hot sauce. It tasted better than ever. A little milk to cover the flames, a cup of coffee, and he was set for the day.

"Do you fancy a picnic this afternoon?" he asked. He felt that good, and after being in bed for a week, he really wanted to be outside.

"Not a good idea, Clarence. You need to stay in a few more days before you start exerting yourself."

"We can go down to that flat grassy area by the river. It isn't hard walking. We could go mid- to late-afternoon and not stay very long. We'll come back whenever you say." He looked up at her, playfully, pleading. "Please, Mommy!"

"Okay, I'd like to do that. How about some turkey sandwiches and apple salad?"

"And beer." An unattended detail popped into Clarence's mind. "Does Aunt Anne know about my accident? I need to call. That is, if you didn't."

"She knows, although I didn't give all the details. How about if she comes tomorrow and goes to church with us?"

"A great idea, Susan. Thanks for taking care of that."

He had just settled into his favorite overstuffed chair in the den, and started on the morning paper, when the doorbell rang. He heard Susan walking to the door and then, "Come in, Mister James. What brings you out on a Saturday morning?"

"Just a bit of news. Is the Professor...?" He stopped. He had his answer before he finished the question as he came into the den. "Good morning, Professor," James said cheerily. "How are you feeling? You look a lot better."

"Have a seat, Detective. Coffee?"

The detective shook his head. "I've only got a minute. I thought I'd drop by with a bit of news. We've confirmed that this fellow actually did the shooting. I followed your advice. Took him out to the road bank and walked him through the shooting."

"What did he say?" Clarence asked.

"One simple sentence, as he looked down the gun barrel."

"You actually let him hold the gun?"

"It wasn't loaded."

"What did he say?"

"He said, 'It was that Jeep Waggin.' He has brains enough to know what kind of vehicle he was shooting at."

"What else did he know, Detective?" Susan asked. "Did he know who he was shooting?"

"No way, Mrs. Harris. He was just sitting on that bank waiting for the moment. No one in particular."

"But you will hold him, won't you, Detective?" she asked

anxiously.

"Sure. He'll be tried for attempted murder, that is, if a judge finds him competent to stand trial, which isn't likely."

"And, what if he's not competent?" Susan continued.

"He'll probably be put into a treatment facility for the mentally impaired. You and Professor Harris don't have anything to worry about. He wouldn't know the Professor from Adam's cat."

"I don't believe Adam had a cat," said Clarence. "It's not in the Bible."

From Detective James came that same chuckle Clarence heard at the end of his last visit to the hospital.

Clarence sighed with relief. "You ought to take some time off, Detective. Quit working on Saturdays, especially now my case is solved."

"Yeah, well, I have to get back to the office. You know, a detective's work is never done."

"Do you have your lottery tickets for this week, Detective?"

"I will have, by the time I get to the office," James said, with that straight, wide smile. "Two for Mattie and two for me."

The Struggle

Clarence lay on a blanket in the shade of a huge beech tree by the river, taking in the blue sky and billowing white clouds. His pain was gone – as long as he remained still. The beer and sandwiches were just right and he felt completely at ease. This was the most relaxed he had felt in weeks. Susan seemed more relaxed too, she had actually dozed off. He let his mind drift among his favorite thoughts. The children, Erin and Ed, must be relieved at the news that he was out of danger. Erin was probably at the movies with Tom, their favorite Saturday afternoon pastime. Some young girl would be sitting with Christine and Catherine, the twins.

Susan, the girl asleep beside him, was the pride of his life, the source of most of his happiness. He loved her for the order in his life, the excitement of every day, the contentment that made anxiety a rare thing. He loved her for more reasons than he could express. Maybe it was his need, maybe his insecurity. No! It was Susan he loved, not because of some deficiency of his, but her beauty, her grace, strength, self-confidence, commonsense, her order and mastery of her world. Nothing flustered her, scared her or intimidated her. His was not a marriage of equals; it certainly was not male dominated. Susan was the stronger of the two in nearly every way. And he liked it that way, those ways.

"How could I be so lucky," he thought.

Then suddenly he was seized by that revelation again. Compared to the finding and winning of Susan, he was a thousand times more lucky to be living, to have been born. That lucky moment over a half century ago when his mother's and father's genes combined to create him, when his fortune was assured to the exclusion of five hundred million others, had captivated his mind. Life would never be the same again. Sure, he would continue to live and love in Susan's care. Certainly he would cultivate the love and attention of his children and grandchildren, and his love for Aunt Anne would grow. He would continue to teach biology and study birds, especially hawks. *But his life would never be the same.*

He could never again take life for granted. Everything in his future would be measured against what he now knew was an overriding miracle, an unbelievable beginning, a five-hundred-million-to-one triumph. He could never again consider his health, financial security, job goals, or even family in the same light. He now saw that life, even when shortened by disease or accident, was the greatest gift. As precious as the love, security and satisfaction of his life were, they paled in comparison to the gift of life itself.

As a biologist, he knew something about life and its value.

He had read the theories about the beginning of life on earth; the combination of inorganic chemicals aided by lightning or some other source of energy to form the first life-forming molecules in that "primordial soup" where life began. He knew well the biblical story of creation. He also knew the controversy about the creation of life on earth by God, each creature in its present form, against the evolution of creatures from the simplest to the most complex humans. It was a storm he had followed fairly closely.

Even though he knew the arguments well, he was not very moved by them. Long ago he had decided that theology could be very simple or very complicated. In its basic form it could be settled by answering a simple question. "Did humans create themselves?" After this question was answered, all the rest was about the nature of God. For him, the Christian faith was complete and sufficient. Everything didn't have to be explained in human terms. God was not limited by human interpretation. The creation he had come to know about through a career in biology, and a life in church, was miraculous by any description.

His immersion in the mysteries of life was interrupted by movement in the sky, a hawk high above the trees sailing in wide circles, checking out the fields and woods below. He thought about the hawk's nest over near the bypass, and about how long it had been since he looked it over. Actually, there was a nest near here, a broad-winged hawk with two nestlings, he guessed. Maybe that was the one he saw high above the trees.

He'd like to go check on it, but he'd not brought any of his gear, and anyway he couldn't struggle through the pain. He was still some healing away from taking up his favorite work and avocation again, but not much.

* * *

Monday morning was a happy time for Clarence. He was glad to be back at the University office. Susan drove him, although he probably could have managed, since it was his left arm that was still nearly immobile. Susan needed the car anyway to drive to the church to do her volunteer work for Meals on Wheels. Sometimes it fell her turn to use her car for deliveries.

As she dropped him off, she kissed him, and said "Please take it easy, Clarence, and call me if you start feeling bad or tired."

He spent way too much time saying hello to the secretaries, the Department Chairman and fellow faculty, explaining the accident, the shooting, the recuperation, and "How are you feeling?" When he finally got settled behind his desk an hour and a half later, he started preparing for class in the afternoon. Surprisingly he found himself finished by 10:30, and leaned back to reflect on the week past and the one ahead. There was very little mail, and only a few telephone messages that required immediate answering.

He found himself thinking again about the question that Ben Carter had asked, and the answer that had struck him so hard. He needed to talk to someone who might help him size up the significance of this thing that was taking up so much of his time. Was he making too big of a deal of it? Was there anyone who had wrestled with the miracle of conception as he was doing? Surely some of the hundreds of doctors who studied and practiced in reproductive biology had contemplated the probabilities. What did his pastor think of this miracle? All his life he had heard not an inkling of it in church.

The best place to start, he knew, was a talk with Moses Quintos. "Moses," he said aloud, "and what an appropriate name."

Moses was an acquaintance in the Department of Religion and Spirituality, or whatever the name was. Clarence couldn't remember exactly. He'd talked to Moses a few times, the only person on campus he had ever discussed religion with, at least seriously. He looked up his number, reached for the phone and dialed. Professor Quintos' answering machine picked up.

Clarence thought about hanging up and waiting until Moses was in. He didn't like talking to answering machines. In his everyday voice he said, "Moses, this is Clarence Harris. It's not urgent. Just something on my mind. Could you call when you have time? Two-six-three-oh-oh-one-six. Thanks."

At five after one, Clarence walked into the Biology 101 classroom. Most of the students had already gathered. The substitute instructor, an upper-level graduate student, had in a week advanced from the third lecture on genetics to the second in a series on energy. In this series, subjects ranged from the capture of energy by green plants in photosynthesis, to the use of energy by plants and animals for growth, maintaining body functions and, in the case of animals, movement or work. The theme of energy from the sun driving all activity on earth usually kept the students' attention.

The class went really well. The students seemed glad to have him back. He felt comfortable with the subject, interaction with the students was easy, and he was pleased at the interest they showed. He felt comfortable with the class, but not his body; it showed the effects of the wounds he still suffered from.

At the end he made a point of staying around so he could get the attention of Ben Carter when he was more or less alone. He approached Ben just as he went into the hallway. "Ben, could I see you for a minute?"

Ben looked around surprised. "Sure, Professor Harris." He back-pedaled a couple of steps, looking nervous.

"You asked me a question after class, when I was last here just over a week ago."

Ben looked even more surprised. Clarence knew immediately that Ben had forgotten, and that for him the question was unimportant. "You asked how many sperm a man produced during the sex act."

"Oh yeah," Ben said, now really nervous. "Yeah, I remember."

"Well, you won't believe how many. Five hundred million." Clarence emphasized every number.

Ben's eyes widened. He half-turned, a puzzled frown on his face. Clarence expected some expression of wonderment, but instead Ben said, "Thanks Professor. I gotta go, somebody's waiting for me."

Clarence glanced down the hall to the water cooler and saw a cute, short brunette. She looked sixteen. Ben was a lot less interested in the new revelation than in his own attractive companion.

What could have prompted Ben's question in the first place? Surely Ben had a reason for asking it. Perhaps he'd glimpsed the significance of the sperm number. But, no! Perhaps it was just curiosity, perhaps fodder for a dormitory bull-session. Whatever it was, it didn't captivate Ben like it did Clarence.

Back at the office, he noticed his answering machine blinking. He pressed the m*essages* button. The first message said without any identification, "Not too much fun on the first day, Albert." Susan! He knew from the voice, the message, and the endearing name. Then, "Call me when I need to come pick you up."

The second message was from Moses Quintos. "Hi, Clarence, I got your message. Call me back. I'll be in the office the rest of the afternoon."

Clarence picked up the phone and pushed the redial button. Moses picked up on the second ring. "Moses, it's Clarence Harris. Thanks for calling me back... Yeah, I'd like to chat with you about something... Now? Well, I'm not up to walking very far, but if we could meet somewhere... Sure, the Owl's Nest is fine. Thanks. See you in fifteen minutes."

The Owl's Nest was a snack bar in the middle of the campus, about three minutes' walk from Clarence's office. Over the door was a wooden carving of the likeness of an owl's head with exaggerated large eyes. The name probably came from some campus character's idea of a gathering of the wise. He left his office and was there ten minutes before Moses arrived.

A few students were sitting at tables having a mid-afternoon snack of soft drinks, crackers, peanuts, and candy bars. It was a small informal social gathering, noisy, but nothing like when it was full of students. A few faculty came occasionally; none were here today.

Clarence stood as Moses walked to meet him. "Man, what happened to you?" Moses said, when he saw Clarence limping badly on his bruised knee.

"Hey, Moses. Something you wouldn't believe."

"Yeah, I do believe it. It's been all over the news. I'm sorry you got caught in it."

"Well, it's mostly over now. Could have been a lot worse. But what I wanted to talk to you about has nothing to do with my accident."

"So that's what you call it? An *accident*?"

"Yeah. Say, do you think it's too loud in here?"

"Do you want to talk in private?"

"No, it's nothing like that. I just don't want us to have to shout."

"We can go outside and sit in the shade. It's pretty comfortable out there."

Clarence nodded. "Good idea. Do you want a coffee, soft

drink or something? I'm buying."

"Coffee in a paper cup. Thanks."

Clarence bought himself a Coke and Moses a cup of coffee, and they went outside. "Moses, I'm curious. How did you get that name? You're the only person I know called Moses."

They found a bench in the shade, almost hidden from the foot traffic that came by occasionally. It was cool with a slight breeze, ideal.

"Completely ordinary in Latin America," Moses said. "Where I'm from there are lots of Moses. We spell it and say it a little differently. M-o-i-s-e-s. Like Moises Alou, you know, the baseball player."

Clarence understood instantly. Moses didn't look very Latin, but now it was clear. He had noticed a slight accent that surely must have come from one of the Latin American countries. "Oh, yeah, sure, I never made the connection. But listen, Moses, I want to ask you some questions. You may think them strange, or weird, or just trivial."

"Listen, Clarence, I specialize in the strange and weird."

"Well, I want your opinion and maybe some support for an idea that came to me. It's taken over my mind."

"Just the kind of ideas I deal with. Some of them take over *my* mind."

Such flippant remarks made Clarence suspect that Moses might not take him seriously, even though Moses hadn't heard a word of his problem yet. "What do you consider the miracle of birth?" he asked.

Moses hesitated. Clarence could sense the thinking ahead, the plotting, anticipating what Moses must be doing to make his answer fit with whatever came next.

"It means many things, Clarence. The formation of a new human being 'in God's likeness', the creation of a soul, a personality. For the parents, fulfillment of a dream, though sometimes it can be a nightmare if the child is unwanted or deformed. But in most cases it extends the parents, gives them a feeling of immortality. They know they won't live long on this earth, and it's comforting to know that they'll live on in their children. I know that's a feeble start, but let's hear your idea."

"No, Moses, it's a good description. I think the miracle, in most people's minds, is the birth process, the formation of a human body. I like yours better. But I came to a realization somehow, I'm not sure how, of a part of the miracle that I have never considered before. And I've never heard or read about it."

"Are you going to tell me? Or are you going to keep it to yourself?" Moses said with a grin.

"Well, of course you know the conception process. What you may not know is the improbability of conception."

"Not so improbable. Happens all the time." Moses was still grinning.

Clarence felt irritated. He wasn't being taken seriously. Maybe this was the reaction most people were going to have to this miracle: *Happens all the time.* "No, I mean at the moment of conception the egg is surrounded by five hundred million sperm. The chance for a given sperm to fertilize the egg, say the one that combined with your mother's egg to create you, is about one in five hundred million. That's the only chance that you had of being born."

"But if the conditions were right that day," said Moses, "the chances were pretty good that *someone* was going to be conceived."

"You're right, but except for that one-in-five-hundred-million chance, it wouldn't have been *you*. So the miracle of conception that happened that day was not for the parents. As you say, the chances were good that a child would be born. The miracle was not for the human race; that miracle happens thousands of times a day across the world. It isn't a miracle in the usual sense of the word. The miracle was for the child that would emerge in nine months. His chances were one in five hundred million."

Moses stayed silent for several seconds. Clarence was determined to wait him out.

Finally Moses spoke. "You're right. I never thought of birth or conception in that way."

"Is it unknown in theology? Surely someone has considered it before. The Christian church has celebrated birth as long as there's been a church, and still does. But has *this* aspect been considered? The enormous number of sperm is a biological detail unknown a century ago. Is it important or trivial?"

"Yeah — what did you say the chances were? How many sperm are there?"

"About five hundred million sperm per time, per sex act – a

half billion."

Moses closed his eyes in thought. "That seems like an astronomical number. Is it really that high? That's more sperm than there are people in North America!"

"I know."

Moses was quiet for longer this time. Then he said, "The chances are even smaller than you say. If the odds against the individual at conception are five hundred million to one, the odds against his or her parents were the same at their conception — before their birth."

"That's right," Clarence agreed. "The odds of you being the winner at the time of conception are one in five hundred million. But, as you say, the odds are much less than that, because each of your parents had the same small chance of conception. In fact, the odds against are multiplied, not added. A simple example would be to think of the odds of the single dot on a dice representing the odds of each of your parents being conceived, that is, one in six."

"So, six sperm for each egg; six sides to the cube," said Moses.

"Yes, but the chance of snake eyes, with two dice, is not one in six or even one in twelve, but one in thirty-six, the square of the number of sides on one dice. Likewise, the chance that both of your parents would be conceived is not one in five hundred million, but one in the *square* of five hundred million."

"Yeah? What is that number?"

Clarence was ready, having calculated it soon after seeing

the mind-boggling number of sperm in the medical handbook. He said slowly, "One out of two hundred and fifty quadrillion!"

"No kidding! Quadrillion? Tell me what a quadrillion is."

"A thousand trillions," said Clarence.

"That means that the probability of both my parents being born is nearly zero," said Moses quietly. "And if either of them had lost out in the race of the sperm for the egg, my chance would have been zero. But if I want to calculate odds, I have to include the odds of the parents being conceived, and the grandparents, and other ancestors, *ad infinitum*. And even in the first two generations back, the odds become so small that they are meaningless. One might say trivial. And the chances of your ancestors, male and female, meeting in the first place have to be factored in. Most husbands and wives meet by chance. If one set of your great, great grandparents hadn't met, or if one of them had a headache instead of sex on the night your grandparent was conceived, your chances would definitely have been zero."

Clarence had already thought of it. "Well, another way of summarizing all of this is by saying that the odds of being conceived are zero, right?"

"Practically speaking, yes."

"Not a ghost of a chance, right? But here we are!"

"Right," said Moses.

"It's a miracle."

"You bet. The beginning of a life."

"So, Moses, what do I do about this obsession?"

"What do you want to do about it?"

"I want to forget about it if it's trivial, if it doesn't mean anything. But if it's the miracle I think it is, I want to hang on to it, celebrate it, tell other people about it"

"So you want *me* to tell you which it is?"

This guy answers my questions with questions. He must be a frustrated shrink, Clarence thought. Is it because he has no answers, or because he wants me to do the work, hunt for the answers? Aloud, he said, "I'd like to know if it's important. I'd like someone who is expert in spiritual matters to tell me it's a miracle."

"Do you learn from your pastor, get your answers from him? Tell me, Clarence, did you learn about your salvation from your church? I don't know your position on abortion; but did you learn it from your doctor, your minister, your mother? I suspect your convictions on those and most other religious, ethical and life issues came from your own brain, along with influence from those sources and a hundred others. I'm not an expert on conception and our, that is, religious, attitudes toward it. It's as much a biological issue as a spiritual one. Clarence, you're more of an expert than I am. You've thought a lot about it."

Clarence felt disappointed, but he could understand Moses' reaction. He couldn't blame him for his answers. Perhaps there were no good answers.

Moses looked up suddenly. "Let me tell you one of the problems with your question."

Well, now we're getting somewhere, Clarence thought.

"It seems to me you've already said it's trivial. The odds in favor of your conception were unbelievably low. The fact that you made it is a miracle to you. But for most people it won't rise above the horizon, won't even enter their mind. If it does, it will be fleeting. They won't think about it for a 'New York minute', as some people like to say."

"But they ought to see it" Clarence protested. "They put their money into a lottery with impossible odds. Wouldn't they feel blessed if they won the big jackpot, eighty-five million dollars, or whatever it is?"

"They see the fortune, not the odds. You can explain the odds to them, but they still only see the chance of riches. If people really understood the odds, and accepted them rationally, the lottery would dry up."

Clarence agreed. "They don't know they have already won a lottery richer than any they can buy tickets for, and with odds against them that only God can calculate. It sounds as if you think mine is a revelation to be kept under a bushel."

"Careful what you call it, Clarence! And, if you have a choice between being a kook and a failure, don't choose both."

What faction of the Department of Religion and Spirituality does this guy belong to? Clarence wondered silently. This sounds like a Moses pop-culture proverb.

"You think about it, Clarence. Give it two or three weeks to incubate. Maybe it will hatch, maybe not. What's overwhelmed you are the incredible odds. But it's like contemplating the edge of space. It's so far away nobody can see it, measure it, or even imagine it. The average citizen's life is untouched by it, but the astronomer is obsessed by it."

Clarence just stared, saying nothing.

"Sorry, Clarence, have to go. Lots of paper piled on my desk. I really have enjoyed our talk. Don't look so miserable. You've given me something to ponder that I've not thought of before."

Clarence stood up slowly and held out a hand. "Before you go, Moses, tell me this. Do you think God chose *me*, chose *you*, to be born?"

Moses shrugged noncommittally, but his eyes sparkled with life. He grinned broadly. "Clarence, we could ponder that one for the rest of our lives and get no answers. But there's one thing we *can* know: the Lord loves us and died for us, to bring us close to Him for eternity."

Clarence nodded slowly. "Maybe there's some special thing He wants me to do," he said quietly.

"Yes, Clarence, there may well be."

Clarence smiled. "Thanks for that, Moses. I'm glad you took the time to listen." He stood straighter than he had for a long time. "You've been more of a help than you probably realize."

"Let's do it again sometime," Moses said. Then he was gone.

Clarence sat back down on the bench for a few minutes longer. When he looked at the time he jumped up too quickly, winced at the pain, and headed back to the office. On the way he thought about what had just taken place. Should he make some notes before calling Susan to pick him up? Had he learned enough to justify notes? When he reached the office, he called Susan then sat down at his keyboard and typed deliberately and sporadically in deep and somber thought. He could use the injured left hand a little.

He seemed to have only got started when a knock on the door told him Susan was here. Time had flown by. Looking at the screen he realized he'd actually completed his task. He quickly saved the file and rose with a tremendous burden lifted. He greeted Susan with an emotional kiss that seemed to surprise her. Maybe it surprised them both.

Last Day of Class

Today was going to be a day of commencement, a starting, and a change that had no foreseeable end. Everything was right about it. Clarence had experienced an epiphany. He was changed and he knew it. The change didn't come from some outward force. No emotional eruption, no blinding vision like Paul saw on the road to Damascus, no near-death catastrophe.

What had happened on the bypass could be invoked to make the conversion more dramatic, but Clarence knew it wouldn't work. It wouldn't work because he didn't believe it. This blessing of his life came from the putting together of facts that in themselves were not remarkable. He already knew them — not the numbers but the facts — and had known them for a long time.

As often happens, the fitting together of known facts in new ways produced an uncommon awareness. He felt blessed to a profound degree. The blessing was no greater than that of about seven billion other people currently living on the planet, except he had the extra blessing of understanding. Nothing intensifies gratitude like understanding.

The understanding and gratitude were what would define him from now on. Today's lecture would be different because he was different, and because his perception of the world, including biology, was different. How to summarize? How to expose himself without preaching? How to say what he had learned without sounding bizarre or cultish? How to keep from breaching the ban on religious offerings in public institutions, or offending the students?

Well, he had to do it. He had to follow his current circumstances, and deal later with the result. So when he stepped to the podium and looked into the now-familiar faces, he was ready. For about thirty minutes he gave the class most of his normal summing up. Then he gave his new summary, trying to repeat as little as possible.

"Biology is a study of us and all our fellow creatures. It describes us from atoms to populations. It describes how we move, how we survive, how we affect each other, how we live — but in a physical way, not social. Part of biology is the story of energy. We study how plants capture energy from the sun, how animals get energy from plants. We study the chemical reactions that transfer energy from inanimate objects, like plums and pineapple, to muscle cells that enable us to walk, talk, think and sing. We study vitamins and minerals and other so-called co-factors that help some chemical reactions run.

"We study how plants and animals react to their surroundings: temperature, light, nutrients, stress, even gravity. In extensions of biology we study how these creatures react to diseases, injury, competition, psychological urges and social influences. Some even study the influences of human intellectual exercise, religion and spirituality on well-being of humans.

"Another part of biology is genetics. Genes contain information that is passed from one generation to the next to define how we look, how we act, and how we live. One can escape the conditions of his or her childhood if they are unpleasant, unhealthy or dangerous, but a genetic legacy is inescapable.

He paused for a moment to let his words sink in, and for students to catch up their notes. He smiled as he continued.

"One of the broad principles in survival of many species is the over-production of young; that is, in some species, the birth or hatching of millions, few of which survive. One pair of the ordinary housefly would produce in one season an unbelievable number of offspring if all lived and reproduced normally." He wrote the number on the chalkboard:

191,000,000,000,000,000,000.

"I don't even know the name of that number," he said. "Anyway, it's one hundred, ninety-one times ten to the eighteenth power. A single weed may produce more than a million seeds. It is a blessing for us that only a few of these pests survive to adulthood."

This brought some genuine laughter.

"It is even more of a blessing that we – each of us — survived the process of conception. Our beginning, our conception occurred against unbelievable odds. You probably don't remember the question Ben asked early in the semester about how many sperm were produced by the man in the sex act. It was an important question; important far beyond Ben's imagination. The enormity of the answer to that question has possessed me since Ben asked it. At the moment of your conception, if your father was average, there were five hundred million sperm available to fertilize your mother's egg cell. You are the result of a one in five hundred million chance. You won a lottery larger than one with a ticket for every person in North America.

"We — you and I — were the chosen seed in the winnowing of genes that could have swept us as chaff to the winds of the lost forever. The legion who never were. How could we be so lucky? Was it luck? If you grasp the significance of this final lecture, it will be more important than any other in this course. I wish for each of you success on the final exam, a pleasant and productive summer, and most of all, comprehension and celebration of your amazing fortune of birth."

The Hawk's Nest

This was the kind of day Clarence lived for. Sunny, cloudless early summer, with temperatures set to rise to the mid-eighties. This was the perfect time to look all day for hawks, make notes and take photos. He was trying to document a change in hawk populations in this area of the county that had been converted from mainly small farms, with little woodland, to forests and suburbs. He thought from observations that there were more hawks now than eighteen years ago, when a graduate student had counted hawks in the same area for a thesis on hawks and habitat. That student had not only counted hawks, but using aerial photographs had calculated the percentage of land covered by cultivated fields, forests, idle or non-cultivated farm land, pasture land, and land taken up by buildings, roads and parking lots.

The increase in forests and even wooded lots in subdivisions provided better habitat and more small animals and birds. Better habitat and more prey should produce more hawks. Without systematic counts, however, the good news was just speculation.

The terrain was rolling, and twenty years ago one could see from the highest ridges several farms in the distance. Their patchwork of corn, wheat and pastures, and woodlands following the streams, all with different shades of green, was a pleasing vista that he now missed. The straight, tight fences clear of bushes had separated the patches, giving the final touch to an orderliness that characterized the county.

Now, with fewer open fields and so many tall trees near the roads, the view was much more limited. One of the highest ridges, Walton Rise, had three or four hundred acres of old growth forest that had several hawks' nests that he'd studied in the past. He was already half-way to the ridge where he would resume the hawk counts. The census was already nearly half finished and with any luck, and enough days off, he would be through in about three weeks.

It was a pleasant drive and Clarence was anticipating the day's work. He was thinking of one of his favorite spots on Walton Rise. Among the giant oaks and pines was an opening near the crest. In the middle of the opening was a giant oak as tall as any around. He had kept up with four years of nesting by red-tailed hawks in that oak, in a saddle-shaped crotch of a branch near the top.

He would climb that tree and check nesting progress some time in the afternoon. For now though, he was following the procedure the graduate student used eighteen years ago to count hawks. It required stopping at locations described in the thesis and watching for one hour and counting the number of hawks seen, then tallying them by species. In some locations none were seen, in others there were several. By visiting seventy-five locations in the area twice, over a two-month period, a representative sample of hawks could be counted.

After making two counts in the morning, he went to his favorite spot on Walton Rise to eat his lunch: a salami sandwich, a can of Coke and an apple. He lay back against a large tree trunk at the edge of the clearing as he ate. He watched the top of the tall oak in the middle of the clearing where the hawks' nest was, but saw no sign of nesting.

A small brown creeper was skipping along the trunk near the nest looking for bugs in the bark, making Clarence suspicious that the hawks were not present now or in the last few days. The little sparrow-sized creeper would be in danger so close to an active nest.

Clarence finished his lunch, put the waste paper and Coke can back in the lunch bag and stood up. He threw a couple of pieces of bread and apple core into the bushes for the birds, field mice or whatever. It was time to check on the hawk nest in the big tree. He was fearful that the hawks had abandoned it; he had heard none of their cries nor seen any clues of them since he started eating. That brown creeper was not a good sign.

He put on his climbing gear, testing the spikes on his shoes against the base of the big oak's trunk, kicking against it to see if the spikes were sharp and tight on his boots. He checked his pockets for his knife, notebook and pencil. Last he slipped his small digital camera into the thigh pocket on the left leg of his pants, and slipped his arms through the straps of his small backpack. Maybe he would need it to bring down things of interest. He often did.

He began the climb toward the nest. As soon as he lifted his foot off the ground he heard what sounded like thunder in the distance, but not far in the distance. Thunderstorms had been predicted for late in the day, but he hadn't thought about it since leaving home early this morning. He hadn't noticed clouds as he drove in this morning, but of course on these roads, with forests closing them in, the horizon was not visible. As soon as he got about three-fourths of the way up the tree he'd be able to see, through the gaps in the taller trees, where and how dark the clouds were.

He considered himself an expert tree climber. He climbed regularly growing up, checking for all kinds of creatures, looking for distant places, and often just to be climbing. It was an ideal pastime for a child with no siblings, much unscheduled time, and parents that did not fear unsupervised play. In those days he had no equipment, but could climb nearly any tree with low limbs, and even with no limbs if the trunk was small enough for his bare feet to clamp onto it beneath him. He would draw his feet up beneath his buttocks, place the soles of his feet tight against opposite sides of the trunk and push himself upward. Among his friends, who often went into the woods with him, he'd been by far the fastest up a tree.

Now he climbed more like a power company lineman, using hard downward thrusts into the trunk to set the spikes on the inside position of the soles of his boots. The belt was a safety device in case of a slip of the hand or foot. Then the belt would tighten around the tree and prevent him from falling, but it wouldn't prevent scrapes and bruises as he fell far enough to tighten the belt.

He reached the first break in the canopy and looked out over the trees toward the west. He could see a dark bank of clouds approaching, and a bluish-gray curtain of rain underneath. Heavy rain, if the look was an indication. It was close enough that he knew he was likely to get wet before he returned to ground. He still had several minutes to get to the nest. Notes had to be taken, a photographic record made, and then a few minutes for descent.

Getting wet didn't bother him. He could protect his notes and camera with the zip-lock bags he carried for that purpose. What bothered him was the possibility of lightning. Just the possibility, not the probability. He had never personally known of anybody getting struck by lightning. The probability was tiny, precisely because so few people got hit. Still he worried because of the awesome power he saw in it — and of course there *was* a possibility.

He was almost up to the hawks' nest, and still there was no sign of its occupants. One last limb to climb over and then he could set his spikes in the trunk, put his safety belt around the trunk just below the big fork in which the nest lay, and examine the contents.

What he saw was unbelievable. The nest was covered by the reddish-brown feathers of the mother's lifeless body. He reached gingerly for it, holding his hand just above the body and laying it down gently. There was no warmth there. He reached underneath and nudged it upward enough to see a chick that couldn't have been more than a week old. The movement made its tiny head pop up and the mouth fly open in an instinctive reach for food. It appeared to be healthy but weak.

His heart sank at the sight of the days-old orphan. Reaching a hand underneath both sides of the mother, he lifted the lifeless body and saw a second chick, dead. He let the big hawk down, raised one side higher, reached in with his other hand and took the lifeless chick out of the nest. It looked normal, except its beak and the front of its head was gone, blown away.

Almost instantly he knew what had happened. He stuffed the chick in the thigh pocket on his canvas-duck pants and lifted the mother hawk and turned it over. A small caliber bullet had passed through the body, embedding fragments of straw and other nest material in the feathers around the entry wound. He examined the nest and saw no evidence of a projectile entering it. But on the opposite side and underneath, a slight grazing of the supporting limb was a tell-tale sign of the bullet that had mortally wounded the chick and its mother. The shooter probably concluded that the nest was empty, because the hawk was killed instantly and never fluttered out of the nest.

The Overriding Miracle

Clarence was suddenly in a rage about the senseless killing of birds of prey. It was an emotion he'd felt many times before. The first was when he was about twelve at his grandfather's house. Grandpa Harris kept chickens in the extended backyard of his house on the edge of town. Clarence's mother had just dropped him off at Grandma's house that Saturday morning, and Grandpa was out back with a shotgun. Grandma told him he couldn't go out because Grandpa was "taking care of that chicken hawk."

Clarence went to the big window in the dining room that looked out onto the back yard just in time to hear the gun go off. When Grandpa came up to the house carrying a hawk by its feet, Clarence yelled at him in pain and rage. He went into a three-day sulk, having nothing to do with his grandfather in spite of favors lavished on him to regain his affection. Neither Grandpa nor Grandma Harris could understand the trauma inflicted on him by the shooting. Neither could he.

Since then he had learned enough about birds of prey to know that their persecution years ago on farms was both understandable and unwarranted. He had found out that hawks seldom made off with baby chicks or other domestic animals. Anyway, chickens could be protected easily by putting young ones in houses of runs covered with chicken wire.

Even the pretense years ago for shooting hawks was no longer valid. This hawk was shot for sport. No, not even sport. This was wanton shooting of a nest without regard for what was in it, or whether good or harm came from it.

He didn't know how long he had been stewing about this dead hawk, when his mind came back to the present. He had to get the live chick down from this tree and see if he could save it. There was nothing he could do for the dead mother and chick, so he returned the dead chick in his pocket to the nest. He pulled feathers from the mother's underside and lined his small backpack. He placed the live chick among his mother's feathers and carefully put the pack over his shoulders where the chick would be safely on his back. He photographed the nest along with a number on a card he had previously assigned to it, and made a note that the hawk family had been destroyed by a gunner.

As he started down he realized that the thunderstorm was upon him, and he was likely to get soaked before he could reach his truck. He was halfway down the limbless lower trunk when the one chance in a million happened. A bolt of lightning struck the big oak, shattering bark from top to bottom. Clarence and the little hawk didn't have a chance.

So the human life that began against impossible odds, and was nurtured secretly by a compassionate aunt known as "Mama", was ended by an act of God against incredible odds. The demise of Clarence Harris was certain; only the time and circumstance were incredible. The real miracle was that he ever existed.

Retrospection

Susan Harris walked down the long avenue of trees leading to Clawson Hill cemetery. It was her weekly pilgrimage to a spot where she could best locate her memories of Clarence. For six months after the funeral she had made it every day, and every day it tore her heart. It didn't help relieve the pain, it likely increased it. Her hardest times were here.

She would stay for half an hour alone, throat constricted with grief the whole time. And the tears came uncontrollably. She was reliving the funeral daily. Her friends tried to distract her by invitations to dinner, to shop, to movies. It didn't help.

She knew that people who knew her as a calm and level-headed woman would never have suspected her of such weakness. She could hardly believe it herself, but she was completely unprepared for the loss of her husband. She never realized how much of her life was invested — no, grafted was a better word — in Clarence. She never considered him an especially strong man. Steady, but not strong. Now she knew he had held her together, erased her worries, filled her inner space to a degree she could not have imagined. Her life had fallen to pieces, and she only kept it together by following the habits of her married life as best she could without him.

She realized that she had come to know Clarence in their last year in a way she had not before. Their intimate conversations had been mostly about themselves and family, current problems, happiness. They had never shared philosophical views or understanding, had not discussed closely-held religious views.

She knew now that something had changed in Clarence. She had been surprised when he confessed his being overwhelmed by the astonishing good luck of being born, and was just as surprised when Moses Quintos recently told her about Clarence's discussion with him. The experience must have been something equivalent to a Christian conversion, a revelation of the power and goodness of the Almighty.

She had been further moved by a file she found on Clarence's computer that George Stoddard had brought to her home several weeks after the funeral. He had brought it because some of Clarence's personal files were on there, and he wanted her to have them and search for others that might be personal or helpful. The files could have been downloaded to a disc and given to her, but George said he didn't want anyone else going through them. She was unappreciative of this precaution simply because she didn't understand the implications.

The file that convinced her of the depth of Clarence's conversion was labeled *Blessing*. When she first opened it she believed it was something Clarence had found and copied from another source, perhaps to use in a Sunday School class or devotional. It seemed so unlike him, a written prayer entitled *Primal Blessing*. She forgot about the file for months. It was the least of her concerns. However, after talking to Moses and reassessing the depth of this experience, she remembered it. She went back to the computer and looked at the file properties. She noticed the date. *Created March 13*. This year. "That's near the time of his accident," she said aloud.

She opened Clarence's calendar file on the computer and went to the date. Two appointments were noted, *Biol. Lecture — Energy* and *Moses Quintos — after class*. Even the time of creation of the file was given in the File Properties Menu — 4:56 pm. Thinking back, she realized that this was Clarence's first day at work after his accident. She'd picked him up because he was too sore to drive and his Jeep was wrecked.

She couldn't remember what time she picked him up that day, but it must have been around five o'clock. So Clarence had written this prayer! It had to be! He had just discussed his new revelation with Moses Quintos, and by Moses' account was extremely moved by it. He would not likely have been looking for passages for a devotional between a discussion with Moses and being picked up around five.

Still, she couldn't believe Clarence had written it. She'd never heard him express such profound joy, faith, and purpose. She closed her eyes. "If there is a special purpose for such an unlikely life, God help me find it!" She had to know — but how? Moses! Maybe he knows more about this than he told me.

Maybe Clarence was more open about his change of life with Moses.

Susan had been standing at Clarence's grave for forty-five minutes, but her mind was still searching the past. She quickly started her car and drove home. As soon as she reached home she looked up Moses Quintos' office number and called.

"Dr. Quintos, it's Susan Harris. I need to ask you something."

Moses seemed to hesitate for a moment. Maybe he didn't know how to address her. "Ms. Harris, how are you? Sure, I'll be happy to help if I can."

"Do you remember a while back, you, I mean we, talked about a conversation you had with Clarence after his accident? When he went back to work?"

"I remember it well," Moses said guardedly, as though sensing the awkwardness Susan felt.

"I have something on Clarence's computer. I'd like to know if he wrote it." Susan was painfully aware of her clumsiness at expressing herself, and the poor preparation for her questions.

"Tell me Ms. Harris, does it have anything to do with what Clarence and I discussed?"

"That's what I want to ask about. It's something like a prayer and... I just don't know."

"Well, Clarence seemed anxious that day about what he'd discovered."

"But I've never known Clarence to write anything like this, or say anything like it."

"Would you like me to look at it, Ms. Harris?"

"Dr. Quintos, I'm sorry to take up your time with such a trivial request, and to call you unprepared to make myself clear."

"I'm sure it's not trivial, Ms. Harris. I'll help if I can. I've not forgotten how deeply Clarence seemed to be affected. What he said even challenged me when I realized the thinness of the thread of existence of individual humans. Your husband had gained a new insight about the creation of human individuals." Moses laughed awkwardly. "What I'm trying to say, Ms. Harris, is would you like to meet and talk? I could meet you somewhere on campus, or maybe you'd rather come by my house. My wife and I would be pleased to have you visit."

It was Susan's turn to be uncomfortable. "I'd like to show you the passage — uh, prayer. Maybe if I came by your office, or I could meet you somewhere on campus. Perhaps I could mail it to you."

Moses seemed to sense her need to see him face to face. "I could meet you this afternoon or tomorrow, whenever you like."

"This afternoon would be fine."

"How about three? We can meet here in my office, third floor of Cox Hall. Do you know where it is?"

* * *

Susan took the elevator to the third floor and stepped across the hall to the departmental office, a large room with a large glass window behind which was a clean desk. A small sign on the desk identified the receptionist as Eve Swain, but there was no one in. Susan's watch and a large wall clock over the desk agreed: she was five minutes early.

Looking at the door numbers, Susan decided Moses' office was to the right coming off the elevator, so she walked that way. The door was open and Moses was seated behind a large desk in a small office absorbed in some papers among the dozens that covered the desk. Susan tapped on the door frame.

Moses looked up, smiled, rose easily and walked to the door. He was athletic-looking, about six-feet-two with broad shoulders, receding black hair and dark eyes, quite Latin. He wore a light gray knit shirt and dark blue slacks. He took Susan's hand in both of his, and said, "It's good to see you, Ms. Harris."

"Please call me Susan."

Moses motioned her to a comfortable office chair in front of his desk. He sat in an identical one, moving it from the front corner of the desk to a position between her and the door.

Susan took the folded paper from her purse, with the passage in question, and handed it to Moses, rising half-way and taking one step forward to reach his outstretched hand. "This is what I thought you could help me with."

Moses smiled again as he took it. A genuine smile containing sympathy. "Susan, I'd like you to know that Clarence is greatly missed among the faculty. People in my department who knew him, and many of my other acquaintances on campus, have talked about the loss to the University. We knew him mostly for his kindness and integrity, his even-tempered approach and love for his work."

Susan had heard the expressions before, but they hurt much more then because of the freshness of the wounds. She appreciated them even more now. "Thank you. Everyone has been so nice."

After an awkward moment, Susan noticed that Moses hadn't unfolded the paper. She pointed to it. "I found this on Clarence's computer that they sent to our house. I would really like to know if he wrote it."

Moses unfolded the paper and read.

Primal Blessing
Untouchable God, what have You done?
You have put me here beyond all odds.
You gave me birth when there was no chance.
You exalted me to existence; a lucky life from a
universe of souls that never were.
Why me, Lord?

Out of uncountable obstacles to life, why me?
From an endless web of biological adventure,
anonymity, and happenstance, why me?
The chance of my conception was small beyond
any calculation, and
You chose me!

> My understanding is as small as my chance of being born, and my gratitude is as small as my humanity.
> But today I have known Your majesty and mystery as never before.
> If there is a special purpose for such an unlikely life, God, help me find it.

"Do you think he wrote it?" Moses asked, looking up.

"I'm trying to decide. I think it's beaut..." Her voice broke momentarily, her lower lip quivered and constricted, but she quickly recovered, partly a quick reaction to embarrassment. "But it doesn't sound like him. I've never known him to write or talk like that."

"Did your husband ever say anything to you about his realization of how lucky he was to be born?"

"He did. It was just after he got out of the hospital, after he was shot by that deranged man and ran off the road. I thought at first he was talking about being lucky to have survived. I could tell he was really moved by it, but I didn't think about it separately from his recovery from the ordeal he'd been through. I was just thankful for his survival."

"Susan, did Clarence talk about being thankful?"

"You mean about survival of the accident?"

Moses nodded.

"I don't know, Moses. As I said, I thought he was talking

about the accident, but now I'm not sure. He talked several times about the unbelievably small odds in favor of being born. He called it the 'overriding miracle'."

Moses studied the paper again. "Susan, is there anything in this prayer that sounds like Clarence?"

She looked up. "Not really. I know Clarence prayed. He prayed aloud in small groups, in Sunday School, at meals. Mostly prayers of thanks, asking forgiveness, blessings. Nothing about the miracle of birth. Nothing as poetic, with as much feeling as those words. Not as much emotion."

Even as she spoke, Susan realized she was starting a new examination that she hadn't done before. She was enumerating the old Clarence. There had been a change, and now she was beginning to see it. She remembered the day he had made his discovery. Hobbled by healing injuries, he had told her his revelation. His face, his unbelieving eyes, the wonder in his voice told her that he knew some miracle. She'd thought it was gratitude for escaping death, but now she could see it was the near unbelief at receiving life, gratitude for a gift that almost no human understands.

She remembered the, perhaps unconscious, sobbing as she held Clarence's head in her lap while he slept soon after his revelation. She remembered the changes she'd seen in him after that day. These changes were probably not obvious to most of Clarence's friends. Even she had missed most of them, or thought them caused by his narrow escape. He had begun walking alone down by the small lake at the edge of their neighborhood in early morning, looking more upbeat and refreshed afterward than she remembered seeing him before.

Suddenly she realized that she was in a conversation about Clarence that had lapsed for some minutes. She didn't know how long. "I'm sorry," she said, focusing on Moses who was still studying the paper she had given him. "I was trying to remember..."

"It's okay," Moses said, looking up. "I believe he wrote it."

She had come to that conclusion just before him, and now felt anxious to leave. If that prayer was Clarence's, there might be other clues on that computer. Why hadn't she looked for them before?

"I believe so too," she said. "Thank you so much for your time, Moses. I really do appreciate it."

"It was my pleasure, Susan. I wish you all the best. Let me know if I can help in anyway." He was already up and extending a hand.

Susan took it and smiled. "Goodbye. And thanks again."

Reflections

Back home Susan sat down at Clarence's computer. If she had so easily found the prayer Clarence typed, there might be other files revealing how he reacted to the miracle he had discovered. She remembered that the file was in a folder labeled *Misc*. She opened the folder again and searched through the list. After opening several with odd names like *Cnotes*, *Mjobs* and *Crooks*, and finding nothing interesting, she found one labeled *ORM*. She opened it and began to read under the title *Reflections*.

> **Reflections**
>
> What am I to do with this thing, this blessing I don't understand? I know it is incredible, but what does it mean? How will it, should it, change me? How do I comprehend it? I cannot really know how important it is to me until I learn what other people think of it. I know what I feel, but I cannot understand it in isolation. I need help. My life has been given a perspective that I was clueless about before, but now haunts me, takes up my time.

This blessing is a problem! All of my adult life I have guarded my time, tried to focus it on productive activities. My daily planner shows that. The jobs don't all get done, and some get ignored when something more urgent or exciting comes up. But I've kept making schedules of even the smallest tasks, and I keep them in my mind, rearranging and editing when necessary. I've always tried to get back on schedule when I find myself drifting or daydreaming.

Now I'm continually daydreaming. My mind is occupied with what-ifs. What if my mother and father (Aunt Anne and whoever) hadn't met? What if they had been apart on the day scheduled for my conception? Why bother? These are unproductive questions. Life is filled with what-ifs.

The larger question is how important is this discovery, and is it worth my time? The second part of the question needs an answer. I can't get it off my mind. It's the real reason for seeing Moses Quintos, that religion expert who didn't help very much. Was that non-committal attitude by Quintos a clue to the importance of the question? Either Quintos thought it was a trivial question, much ado about an everyday occurrence, or he has never read much about it or heard about it. It certainly has not bothered him for very long, like it's puzzling me.

The first thing to decide is, is it significant? I doubt if I can decide that one. I don't have the mind for it. I don't have the knowledge, the background in philosophy, the training in logic. I haven't read the hundreds of volumes that must exist on the beginnings and significance of human life on earth. But is there likely to be an answer there?

Is there a clue in the Bible? I don't remember anything in Scripture that seems to be helpful. What I recall from the Old Testament are the instructions on worship, the nature of God and His relationship to humans, but nothing about the miracle of life. The New Testament teaches about Christ and new life for those saved through Him, not about the miracle of the old life. The answer is not likely in the Bible, unless the answer is that I should forget about my overriding miracle and focus on the future.

Knowledge about the vast number of sperm at the time of conception is modern knowledge, unknown a hundred years ago. The miracle is in the numbers. But it can't be just about numbers. The gift of life would be just as precious and undeserved if there was no lottery of sperm, chance encounters, and hundreds of other happenings that make individual conception so unlikely.

Why has religion — the contemplation and celebration of creation and Creator — taken so little notice of the miracle of conception? Perhaps because it is the nature of humans to focus on the present and the future. The main focus of Christianity is the salvation of the sinner; conversion from a self-centered life of the past to a Christ-centered life of the future. The main celebration is of Christ and conversion of souls to His teachings, but the overriding miracle is the gift of an unconverted soul. (By the way, when do we get a soul? Are we born with it, or do we get it along with our slow realization of what we are at a few years of age?)

What about the billions of humans born to the earth that don't have a clue, no inkling of the blessing of a chance to live on the earth? No concept of the alternative to conception. A morbid anguish often expressed in literature and personal encounters is, "I wish I had never been born." It's hard to imagine such a wish. Life is sometimes hard, and never quite right, but it is difficult to imagine not having it.

The average person never gives a thought to what it would mean never to have existed. At least, I've never heard anyone talk about it. *That's the reason life is taken for granted!* There is no concept of the alternative. Nobody can imagine never having been born. It's difficult to feel gratitude for a gift you can't imagine being without.

So I'm back to where I started. That's the impossible thing about this obsession. As soon as I think I'm making some progress, I'm back at the beginning. Back to the depressing conclusion that life is to be taken for granted, not celebrated.

Surely not! The Christian-Trinity concept of God includes the Father, and the Father's overriding gift to humans is life. There are thousands of other gifts that religious people, not just Christians, give thanks for, but none come close to the value of life.

We unconsciously grade our gifts. We are truly grateful for a disease cured, hardly grateful for one we avoided altogether. We compare ourselves to those who have weaknesses that we think are larger than ours, without gratitude for what their life contributes to us — if nothing more than a favorable comparison. We feel sorry for the cripple, without celebrating his life. We pray for and aid the poor, but we don't thank God that they are living. We pray for the "lost" and their conversion to Christ, without thanking God that they have souls to save.

We complain about our misfortune. I will never again hear those complaints in the same way. Baleful stories of ill health, bad business deals and human failure are miniature blemishes on the glorious complexion of life. I will hereafter think of the forlorn and depressed. "Can't you see the gift you were given?" I will say to the beggar. "You don't know how lucky you are!" I will declare to the perennial cynic, "If you knew your beginning, you would know that now you are in the presence of God. You almost weren't. Celebrate it!"

"Clarence Harris, I didn't know you! How could I have missed this change? How could you have kept so much to yourself? Why did I have to find out after you were gone, by reading from your computer? Now I wonder how much more I didn't know."

After looking through several other files, she found one labeled *Me*. She opened it and found a poem.

My Selfish Prayer
By Clarence Harris

For a rare, exclusive birth,
And life upon this lovely earth,
For hope to gain eternity,
Thank you, God, for me.

R Harold Brown

I'm grateful, God, to have a place
In this lucky, splendid race,
For refuge on a parent's knee;
Thank you, God, for me.

Thank you for the grace to save
My sinful soul beyond the grave;
But thank you for, most of all,
My chance to have a soul.

God, please help me understand
Why You chose this grain of sand
From all the dunes of every sea
And gave this life to me.

God forgive my selfishness,
Help me more to feed it less,
Except to praise your charity –
This self You gave to me.

The Tree of Life, its blessing gives
To every lucky soul who lives
On earth and through eternity.
Thank you, God, for me.

> Clouds of pollen on the wind,
> Slim the luck at journey's end.
> Billions lost — a single tree,
> Thank you, God, for me.

Susan took a deep breath, feeling flabbergasted. Clarence the settled, pleasant, carefree, loving husband! Clarence the bird lover, the local outdoor adventurer, the scientist, the plodder! Where did this introspection and philosophical analysis of self and God come from? This conversion from doer to thinker, from practical, analytical mind to poet: it was so unlike Clarence.

She began screening her remembrances of him, searching for things he said or did that pointed to this new persona. There was nothing she could point to. The Friday night he came home from the hospital and told her about his new discovery was the strongest clue she had. What about the discovery the night before his mother died that she was not really his mother, but his aunt? It certainly appeared to affect him. He seemed angry and confused that night. Didn't want to talk about it.

Clarence seemed to have adapted to both of those events completely. The visit to Aunt Anne's seemed to turn the revelation of his adoption from trauma to delight. He came home from her house that night entirely happy, talking about how much he owed both his mother and Aunt Anne. He said he could never consider Aunt Anne his mother, but he could never repay her for her sacrifice, for giving him up to a wonderful mother and father and for following his life without interfering. He was amazed that Aunt Anne had kept a detailed scrapbook of his life, probably without even her sister knowing.

Clarence's revelation about the improbability of being born apparently had a larger effect on him, but she knew even less about it. Clarence didn't talk about it, except that Friday night and a few references that didn't stand out for her. Perhaps he intended to, but never knew how or never worked up the courage. Perhaps he was just waiting until he'd thought it through, until he was ready, until he had answers to his questions. Perhaps he had been working it out on his keyboard. These writings were the only clues, and they indicated an intense struggle.

So a life was illuminated by a great blessing made known, not by the church, but from God nevertheless, through knowledge of biology and statistics. And that life was reclaimed by the Creator before the light spread beyond its vessel, at least by its own voice. She suddenly felt a great burden.

"No, God, I can't. I have no conviction, no training, no confidence. I can't speak for Clarence or his miracle. I hardly know about his conviction. I only know what I have read from him, and the look on his face when he first knew. Please!"

Susan Harris had a burden. Knowledge of the overriding miracle weighs heavily on the modest mind. But God has His means!

Made in the USA
Coppell, TX
06 January 2022